Nobody's Family Is Going to Change

Nobody's Family Is Going to Change

LOUISE FITZHUGH

• •

A YEARLING BOOK

Published by
Dell Publishing Co., Inc.
1 Dag Hammarskjold Plaza
New York, New York 10017
Copyright © 1974 by Louise Fitzhugh
All rights reserved. For information address Farrar, Straus and
Giroux, Inc., New York, New York 10003.
Yearling ® TM 913705, Dell Publishing Co., Inc.
Reprinted by arrangement with Farrar, Straus and Giroux, Inc.

ISBN: 0-440-46454-4

Printed in the United States of America
Fourth Dell printing—April 1981

MPC

For Lois

The Principal Characters

DRAWINGS BY THE AUTHOR

Willie Sheridan

Emma Sheridan

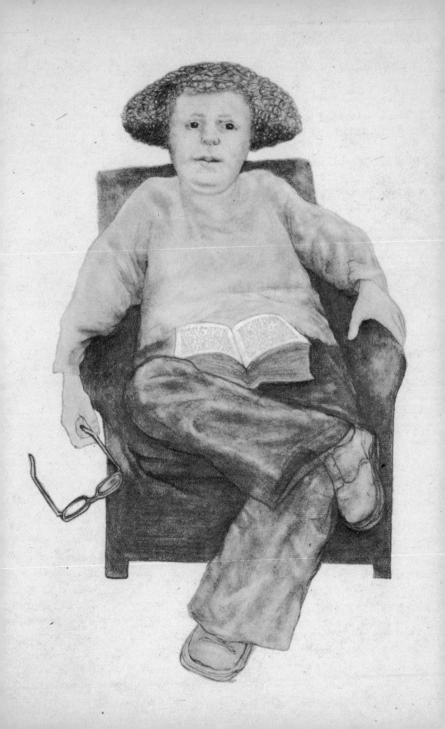

Mrs. Sheridan

Dipsey Bates

Mr. Sheridan

Nobody's Family Is Going to Change

Humming "Me and My Shadow," Willie Sheridan did
a shuffle-ball-change and two flaps as he squeezed out
the toothpaste, then did a soft shoe and brushed his teeth
simultaneously. His older sister, Emma, started her morning complaints outside the bathroom door. He paid no
attention to her, finished his teeth, changed his humming to "Tea for Two" in cut time as he washed his
face, then slowed as he combed his hair. Finishing that,
he put the comb back, turned, did a hop-shuffle step,
saw himself in the mirror, and picked up the rhythm.

"Man, if Bill Robinson was handsomer, he'da looked just like me." He gave himself a big smile and did two pullbacks and a riff.

Emma's voice came loud and clear through the door. "Get your habeas corpus out of the bathroom!"

The door opened and Willie did a buck-and-wing past her through the door.

"Faggot," said Emma right in his ear as he went by.

"I'll punch you right in the hoo-hoo," called Willie over his shoulder as, never missing a beat, he disappeared into his room.

Emma's eyes glowed with hatred as she looked down the hall of the East End apartment after her seven-year-old brother. "Revolting," she muttered to emptiness. She stomped into the bathroom, slammed the door, and gave the same look of hatred to her own reflection in the mirror. She took in, with no surprise, the four brown punching bags that made up her arms and legs, the well-rounded mound of stomach under her striped pajamas, the Afro hair which, for some reason, did not stand up like everyone else's but grew sideways, reminding her of a bird she had seen in the Bronx Zoo.

"Monster," she whispered to herself. "Disgusting. You are truly and completely disgusting." She turned herself sideways to get a better view of her stomach, then advanced to the mirror until her nose touched. Widening her eyes, she tried to take in her own reality. It didn't help. The fat brown girl with funny hair had the audacity to smile at her. "But you're smart. You're smarter than all of them." Before the idiot in the mirror had a chance to retort, Emma thumped away to the sink. "You'll show them all," she muttered through the toothbrush. Brushing as though she had six cars to wash before noon, she began her day.

● ●

Willie missed a step as the bathroom door slammed behind him. He didn't have to see his sister's face to know what it looked like behind the door. He and his father called her Piggy. He liked her, but he was frightened to death of her. She was smart. When she looked over her glasses at him, she could turn him to jelly.

Man, I better hurry, he thought, looking at the clock. I've only got five minutes to practice before Dipsey gets here. One lesson a week. How can I make it on one lesson a week?

He rooted around in the bottom of his closet until he found his tap shoes, jammed them on, threw back the small rug, closed the closet door so he could see himself, and started to work.

He started off real nice and easy with a slow time step, humming "Way down upon the Swanee River," real easy, cool, slow. He speeded up then, did three breaks, and was doing his first buck-and-wing when the door opened quietly.

His mother's face stopped him in his tracks.

"Willie," she said softly, "your father was up until three working on a brief. He goes to court today. You'll wake him up."

"But, Mom, Dipsey's coming and I got to—"

"You can't have a lesson this morning. It's too noisy. I know how much you care . . ."

Willie looked at her in horror.

". . . but it just makes too much noise." Mrs. Sheridan stiffened against what she knew was coming.

"Mom! Dipsey can only come this one time and if we can't do it now I don't have a lesson this week!"

"I know, son, it's too bad, but—" The doorbell rang.

Willie ran as fast as he could to the front door. Mrs. Sheridan followed him. She closed the door to the bedroom hall behind her as Willie let his uncle in.

"Ta, da, ta, da, *da, da!*" said Dipsey and did a big break at the door. "Here's your old dancing master!" He picked up Willie and spun him around in a hug.

"Hush!" said Mrs. Sheridan.

Dipsey said, "Hey, man, how's the old one-two?" before he heard her. "Hi, Ginny!" Then, more softly, he said, "What's the matter, Sis?"

"William is sleeping. He worked late and he goes to court at ten. I'm afraid we can't have any noise this morning."

Two pairs of big brown eyes gave her the same look.

"Oh. Can he miss his first period at school? I could

wait, we could have a lesson and then he could go on to school."

"There's no one to take him there if he misses the bus."

"Oh, I could drop him off in a cab. How about it, Sis?"

"I think," she said slowly, "that we had better have a talk."

"Aw, Mom."

"Uh, oh, this don't sound too good, Willie. Come on, let's go on and get this over with so we can settle down and have ourselves some fun." He had his arm around Willie and he pulled him over to the couch.

Willie laughed. They both sat down and looked at Mrs. Sheridan.

"Don't look at me that way, Dipsey, because you know full well what I'm going to say."

"Uh-huh. Big William don't like the idea of Little Willie here going on the big bad stage."

"Dipsey . . ."

"And furthermore, he don't like it at all that Little Willie even thinking about being a dancer, because being a dancer is something that Big William just don't cotton up to. Fact, he just don't see no point in it nohow, at all, any which way!"

"Dipsey. Try to understand what you'd feel like if you had a son."

"If I had a son that could dance like Willie here, that

boy would have been on the road before his mama got him out of diapers. Because this boy's got it, Ginny, that's what you and William never seem to get. I'm not just talking about any boy. He's really got it, and if that big bull—"

"Dipsey!"

"—bullheaded husband of yours could just see that. Scared you, didn't I?" Dipsey laughed his good laugh.

Willie couldn't believe his ears. He knew how his mother and father felt and he knew how Dipsey felt, but he had never heard it all out in the open like this.

"He's not bullheaded!" Mrs. Sheridan was getting angry. "You're making too much of this . . . this talent Willie has. It might occur to you that it's looking at you that makes William not want his son to grow up to be a dancer."

"What's the matter with me?" Dipsey stared at her openmouthed. He turned to Willie. "You see anything the matter with me?"

Willie laughed, but he was getting nervous. What was the matter with dancing? He had the feeling that if he stuck with Dipsey, Dipsey would win out over everybody —but maybe he shouldn't be wanting to win this fight. Maybe his father knew something that he didn't, something even Dipsey didn't know.

Dipsey got up and strutted around the room. "He couldn't possibly find anything wrong with me!" He did such a funny little step that even Mrs. Sheridan laughed delightedly in spite of herself. He ended up right in front of her, stopped suddenly, and pointed a long skinny brown finger right at her nose. "You know and I know and even Little Willie knows that William thinks Dancing Is Sissy!"

"Well, I'm not sure that's the—"

"Don't you not-sure me this and not-sure me that. You know like you know my name, and I know too, what's bothering old William. Now I ask you . . ." He hunched his shoulders and towered over Mrs. Sheridan. "Am I sissy? Do I really look to you like I'm swishing round here?"

Willie laughed. Mrs. Sheridan began plaintively, "Dipsey . . ."

"On the other hand," said Dipsey in a high, fluting voice as he pirouetted across the room, one hand on his hip, and did a high chorus walk back toward them. "Now some of those gypsies in the chorus, ooooh, Mary."

Mrs. Sheridan stopped herself from laughing and frowned severely at Willie, who was holding his belly and laughing uncontrollably. "That's just the kind of oversophisticated thing that William is talking about that you want to go and expose him to. Look at him. He doesn't even know what he's laughing at." She pointed to Willie, who was still writhing around, giggling.

"He knows, oh mama, he knows. He can't be in school two days in New York City and not know that." Dipsey flopped down on the couch, giving Willie a shove on the head. "Ginny, what's happening to you? You and me used to laugh at William and how stuffy he was. Now you getting the same way."

"Dipsey, I'm warning you . . ."

"Okay, okay, but let's look at this thing sensibly. What is a man? A man does what he wants to do, and if he does it well, ain't nobody going to say he ain't a man. And if what a man wants to do is dance, then he better dance better than anybody. I know, baby, I know because I've lived it."

"You've lived it. That's just my point. It's your life, not necessarily Willie's. And he isn't a man. Really, you're being melodramatic and absurd. He's seven years old."

"And how old was I? You remember? You were there cleaning my ears. How old was I?"

"Three, but Daddy was in show business. Momma and Daddy had an act. It was different! And besides, that's your life. You think you've had a particularly good life? Now, be honest!"

"Honey. It don't matter a bit what you say. I'm just trying to save you a lot of grief. When somebody has got what Willie here has got, they know just where they're going and there's just no point in trying to stop them."

He looked at Willie, who grinned at him. "Where you going, Willie?" he asked.

"Broadway," said Willie, grinning.

"Oh, this is ridiculous," said Mrs. Sheridan. "He's a

child. His mind is being formed this very minute. How can you fill him up with dreams that will hurt when they don't happen?"

"Have you taken a look lately at all those people walking the streets that don't have any dreams? It's better to have a busted one than none at all, and his isn't going to get busted. He's going to make it. Why can't you understand that? Let me have him just this one summer—"

"He doesn't know what he wants, Dipsey. His father wants him to be a lawyer just as much as you want him to be a dancer, and I want him to be happy."

"One summer, just one summer in stock, and after that we'll talk again."

"You know and I know that what his father is worried about has some validity, that if he spends one summer in stock he may never be the same again. Things happen. Think, Dipsey, think!"

Dipsey stood up. He appeared to be leaving. "You know, Sis," he said slowly. "I just got me an idea. I think old William and maybe you are scared to death that this boy here is going to have more fun in life than you're having."

● ●

Emma was standing and looking into the refrigerator when her mother, infuriated by Dipsey's last statement, came into the kitchen.

Emma jumped as though she'd been caught nude.

Mrs. Sheridan looked at the remains of what Emma had already eaten. She looked at her daughter in despair.

"Darling, that's enough for breakfast. You don't want to grow up to be a fat woman. If you keep on like this, it's only going to be much harder when you get older. Why do you do this?"

Emma didn't say anything. Her mother's face was worried, but her eyes were loving. She's looking at me, Emma thought, like I'm a word that doesn't fit the crossword puzzle.

"My teeth were itching," said Emma unexpectedly.

"Darling." Mrs. Sheridan put out her hand to touch Emma's head.

"Ick. Mush," said Emma, and thumped heavily back to her room.

● ●

That afternoon Willie did a fast shuffle down the aisle of the school bus, then a big leap out the door. The other children laughed and waved at him. He did a time step for them until the bus roared away.

He looked up Eightieth Street. The garbage truck was standing at the corner. Charlie, the big fat guy, waved at him and did a funny little tap. Willie did a little tap back like an answer. Nick, the skinny one, yelled, "Hey! Willie!"

Willie danced over to them, trying to wave his brief-case like a straw hat. Charlie emptied a can into the churning back of the truck, dropped it with a clatter, and started to dance like crazy, flopping around and twirling his arms like big pinwheels.

Willie kept up a fast time step, dropped his briefcase, and clapped his hands, humming "Way down upon the Swanee River." Nick slapped down another can, ran over to Charlie, and they did an old vaudeville exit like two hoofers with canes. They were all three shouting the song, screaming and laughing.

Nick came running back from around the truck where they'd disappeared, and started shuffling like a mad thing. "That's a shag, baby, ever seen the shag?" He panted, he was going so hard.

The truck door slammed and the driver came bowl-ing around the side. It wasn't Frank, the regular driver. It was another man, who didn't look too friendly. Nick stopped abruptly and grabbed a full can from against the building.

"What the hell is this, the Ted Mack hour? You guys pick up the garbage as fast as you dance, we get New York cleaned up in a week." He looked angry. Charlie winked at Willie behind the driver's back. Willie picked up his briefcase.

"Who are you?" asked the driver, hands on hips, looking down from six feet.

Nick was next to him suddenly, and Charlie ran over. Nick put his hand on Willie's head. "This my boy Willie. He's going to Broadway!"

"No kidding? This your son?" The driver was smiling now.

Nick laughed. "No. I sure do wish my son could dance like that."

Willie felt an astounding sensation. He wanted to leap, as high as he could, as high as the building. He couldn't even look at Nick.

"All right, come on, guys, let's get it moving." The driver was bored now. He turned his back and started toward his cab.

"Don't worry about him," said Charlie. He jumped up on the back of the truck, his balloon body moving so fast it was surprising.

Nick threw the last can against the building with a satisfactory clamor. "Give 'em hell, Willie!" he yelled as he jumped up beside Charlie. The truck started to move away. Willie stood watching.

"Give my regards to Broad-way," Nick sang above the roar of the truck. Charlie joined: "Remember me to Herald Square . . ." Together: "Tell all the gang at Forty-second Street . . ." They were turning. Now Willie couldn't see the truck. ". . . That . . . I . . . will . . . soon . . . be . . . there" came to him ghost-like from around the corner. Silence was there. Willie felt odd. He walked toward his apartment building.

"Hi zer, Villie," said the doorman, who was of an undetermined Baltic origin. He bore a strong resemblance to Dracula, and his doorman's cape didn't help.

Willie barely heard him. Concentrating, he walked in, smiled absently at the doorman, pushed the elevator button, and walked through the opening doors.

"Ess," said the doorman behind him, breathing through his teeth.

Willie danced wildly, impatiently, by himself in the elevator as it was going up. He felt his feet were making angry sounds.

Old Mrs. Goldstein was waiting for the elevator as he danced out. Tapping in place, he held the door for her. "A regular Fred Astaire," she muttered as she went past him slowly.

The door closed. Willie practiced dancing up the wall as he'd seen Donald O'Connor do in an old movie. It was hard. He went to his own door, fished around for his key, and let himself in. "I'm home!" he yelled.

"Ter-*rif*-ic," he heard Emma say from her room in a deep, sour voice. She slammed her door.

He went into the kitchen, started looking for cookies. "Well, if it isn't Bill Robinson." It was Martha, the maid. She was white and wildly freckled, but Willie liked her. Sometimes she had a sharp tongue that could make him feel like a worm, but she was there to come home to every day, and friendly most of the time.

She gave him a toothy grin. Her teeth stuck out. He jammed a cookie in his mouth and started tapping down the hall to his room. "Here, now, get this book satchel out of my kitchen."

He danced back and got it.

"Can't you even say hello?"

He stopped. He usually said hello. I am going to do something, he thought. I don't know what it is that I am going to do, but I am going to do something and I am going to do it soon.

"Hello." He smiled, then danced out. "Helloooo," he wailed like a ghost as he ran down the hall.

"Between you tappy-tapping and your sister the district attorney, a person could go starkers around here," Martha called after him. Martha was always talking to herself. Martha talked all the time, whether there was anybody in the kitchen or not. He closed the door on her voice.

He flung down his briefcase and ate his cookies to a slow soft shoe in front of the mirror. "If Nick were my father" raced through his head and was stopped like a car at a light. A vision of summer stock rose in his mind, as firm and as sweet as the cookies, pictures of him and Dipsey having dinner at four o'clock because they had to go on at eight and it didn't do to be too full when you danced, pictures of backstage, pictures of footlights blinding and—suddenly he saw his father sitting in the audience, ashamed of him.

● ●

Emma trudged home heavily, her books seeming to weigh more than the day before. She was having a running argument with herself about the consumption of a cream horn, an additional, unnecessary cream horn, at lunch that day. The argument went through her head like this:

THE STATE OF NEW YORK AGAINST EMANCIPATION SHERIDAN

DISTRICT ATTORNEY: Your name is Emancipation Sheridan, otherwise known to your friends and family as Emma Sheridan?

EMMA: Yes.

D.A.: Yes, sir.

EMMA: Yes, sir.

D.A.: Now, Emma, tell the jury what you had for lunch today.

EMMA: Hot dogs and sauerkraut.

D.A. (*snidely*): And what else, Emma?

EMMA: Chocolate milk.

D.A. (*insinuating*): And?

EMMA (*looking down and whispering*): A roll.

D.A.: Now, Emma, you're evading the question.

You realize that you're under oath. Are you going to swear under oath to the honest, upstanding ladies and gentlemen of the jury that that's *all* you had for lunch?

EMMA (*whispering even lower*): A cream horn.

D.A.: What? Speak up. We can't hear you.

EMMA (*a bit louder*): A cream horn.

D.A. (*greatly irritated*): Your honor, will you please direct this witness to answer my questions loudly and clearly so that the court and the jury can understand her?

JUDGE: Miss Sheridan, will you please try to speak up?

EMMA: Yes, sir.

JUDGE: What?

EMMA: Yes, sir.

D.A. (*swaggering around*): Now, Miss Sheridan, will you please tell the jury what else you ate for lunch.

EMMA: A cream horn.

D.A. (*slyly*): Do you want to leave it at that?

EMMA (*yelling*): Oh, all right, *two* cream horns.

Emma almost walked into a parking meter. She stopped herself just in time and trudged along, back in the real world now. Oh, the shame of it. Two cream horns.

Still, when she finally passed her bar exam and she

finally had a case and she was cross-examining the school dietitian, it would go like this:

> EMMA (*prominent young New York trial lawyer*):
> Did you or did you not put out a tray of forty cream horns—and don't say there weren't forty, because there were, because I counted them— did you or did you not put that tray out there to tempt and lead astray and in particular to ravage the diet of one Emma Sheridan?
>
> DIETITIAN (*meekly*): I did.
>
> EMMA: If it please the court, this witness refuses to speak up and I have failed in all my efforts to get her to speak louder.
>
> JUDGE: We will have no more of that. Dietitian of the Gregory School, you *will* speak up.

Emma gave a smile of satisfaction. She watched the dietitian cringe and wiggle around for a minute, then own up to her crime. Her mother's voice broke through her dream: Just because there were forty, that didn't mean that you had to eat forty, Emma. It didn't mean that you even had to eat *one*.

The shame of it. It was nobody's fault but her own that she ate like a horse and looked like a pig, so much so that everybody called her Piggy. At first she hadn't minded. There was a friendly sound to the name. As she got fatter and fatter, however, she realized that there wasn't anything friendly about it. It was merely a descriptive term for that most shameful of all things, a FATGIRL.

Emma gave a little shudder. Rounding the corner, she saw Willie up the block dancing around the garbage men.

How my father ever thinks he can make a lawyer out of that dancing faggot, I can't imagine. Here I am, with one of the best legal minds in the state . . . She drifted toward another courtroom scene but was stopped by her rage as she stood like a lump watching Willie shuffle around with the garbage men.

As she watched, Emma was remembering the conversation with her father that had taken place the night before. Mr. Sheridan had been sitting in the living room reading the paper. Mrs. Sheridan was knitting and watching television, with the sound turned so low that Emma could barely hear it even when she was in the room, standing in front of her father's chair.

"May I discuss something with you?" she asked abruptly. Emma had a fairly deep voice. It made almost everything she said abrupt.

Mr. Sheridan put down the newspaper. "Certainly, certainly," he said jovially. He folded the paper, took his feet off the ottoman, and indicated that she sit down. "What have you got there? History? Algebra?" He was smiling.

"Torts."

He stopped smiling. He didn't look angry, just paler.

"Have you finished your homework?" he asked quietly.

"Yes."

"Where did you get this book?"

"From the library."

"What is your question?"

"In New York State, do you feel there is adequate legal protection of women in cases of rape?"

"Emma!" Mrs. Sheridan put down her knitting.

Mr. Sheridan ignored his wife. "What are you asking?" He looked at Emma.

"The burden of proof seems to be on the woman. She has to have a witness. How many people are going to rape somebody when witnesses are around?"

"That law has been repealed."

"Oh?"

"Didn't know that, did you?" Mr. Sheridan looked immensely satisfied. "At any rate, there was a good reason for that law. The accusation of rape is very grave. A man is being accused of a heinous crime. It cannot be done lightly."

"But he'd have to do it in broad daylight in the middle of the street to get enough witnesses to say— Anyway, *rape* is very grave."

"As I said before, that law has been repealed. Any other questions?" His voice was cold.

"Yes. If a woman is raped by an F.B.I. man, does it

come under federal law?"

"I don't believe the question has ever come up. You would have to look up the law on that."

"Thank you." Emma had said this politely, had picked up her book and thumped away. She had heard her parents' short exchange as she went down the hall to her room.

"Why are you so cold with her?" asked Mrs. Sheridan. "Her questions seem reasonable enough."

"You don't understand. Her questions are those of a law-school student. I sometimes get the strange idea that she could pass the bar exam right now—"

"But aren't you proud?" It was one of her mother's rare interruptions.

"—and *she* thinks she'd get a better mark than I did." Her father finished on a note of despair.

Afraid of me, is he, thought Emma, progressing down the street toward her apartment house, having decided that the best thing to do about Willie was ignore him. Anybody who worked that hard for applause ought to be shook up not getting any.

"But if your daughter is bright and will be a fine lawyer someday, I should think that would make you very happy."

"Women lawyers!" her father had answered with a sneer. "Why couldn't it have been Willie?"

Emma let her mind sift around the pain this had caused and, like a forty-niner panning for gold, came up with a familiar stab. She let herself give way to the stab for a fleeting second as she walked into the elevator, but with the change of light and the motion of ascension she let this turn, as it always did, into the just as familiar but far more comfortable feeling of determined anger.

As the elevator rose from floor to floor, she felt her resolve mount too. I will show him. I will make it clear to him that he has made a mistake.

I will bring it all out into the open, she said to herself, as the elevator stopped at her floor, and as the door rolled back, I will do it tonight. I will tell him that I want to go to law school and that, if he won't send me, I will get a scholarship and how will that make him look to his fat friends in the Bar Association?

● ●

After the vision of his father looking ashamed, Willie stopped dancing. He collapsed on the bed, chewing thoughtfully. He felt terrible. He felt unfaithful to his father. He didn't want to be with his father at all. He wanted to be with Dipsey, or Nick, or anybody who liked dancing. He would have gone off, at that moment, with a perfect stranger. If only a perfect stranger would come to the door, would knock, would enter, would say, "You have a job. Come with me. We can use a dancer like you. These people don't understand. These people are not your kind of people. Come with us," and take him by the hand and lead him away.

There would never be any perfect stranger at the door. He would never come. Dipsey was the only hope he had, and this morning that hope had been pushed right out the window.

He squirmed around on the bed, put his feet up against the wall. He started tapping a little. His mother hated him to do that. There were little black marks where one time he had gotten carried away and tapped like crazy. He did it softly now. It helped him to think.

He hated school with his whole body. He didn't see any point in it at all. He was bad at everything.

When he thought about summer stock, everything made sense. He understood everything about that kind of life. You did your best, your very best, and you worked hard, harder than anybody. Dipsey said that theater people worked harder than anybody else. Dipsey said all those people working in offices didn't know what work was. I'm not afraid of work, he thought. Work was just doing it over and over again until you had it just right. He wanted to work, so it wasn't fair. It wasn't fair when that stupid teacher said that he was just lazy and didn't want to work. He did want to work. What did she know? Dumb broad. He got madder and madder. His feet tapped faster and faster.

"Cut that out or I'll come in there and cut your feet off!" Emma's voice came through the wall.

Jerk. He swung his feet down. Rats. Between his

father and Emma, there was no place to go. Only his mother gave him a little smile now and then as though she knew what he was about, and even she this morning, even she had turned out a fink, just working for his father.

He remembered the guy in the hall at school. He'd been running, dancing and running, tapping a little and running from one class to the other, and this guy had minced past him saying "Get you, Mary," and wig-waggled his ass on by like a dame. Willie lost his temper altogether and tackled the guy, downing him, punching him a good one right in the nose. A teacher had come by and picked them up off the floor. She had threatened to send them to the principal if it happened again.

Thinking about everything, Willie got madder and madder. He never got mad. This wasn't like him, and he realized that, as he continued, nevertheless, to get madder. He got so mad he stood up. My life is being ruined, he thought furiously, and I can't do anything about it. I have no control over it whatsoever. I never get mad. I go along and I take everything anybody gives me until I can't take it any more and that's the way it is today. I can't and I won't. I just won't. I don't know what I'm going to do about it, but I know one damned thing and that is that I am going to do something about it.

The rage and the turmoil and the fury began to express itself and he felt his body turn and he felt his body leap. He felt his body do things he didn't know it could do. He felt a release that was like nothing that had ever happened to his legs before, his arms, even his face; his body turned in a way no body had ever turned. In mid-air, defying gravity, he turned and soared and jumped and leapt and winged up like a porpoise. He leapt so high his head felt the brush of the ceiling, and even this did not stop the flow, the turning of his body. Faintly, he heard Emma begin to beat on the wall, but it did nothing to his leaping. His body went on and on, inexhaustible, doing everything that he had ever wanted to do and everything that no one had ever been able to do before, and then he *was* in mid-air, he turned in mid-air and he was before the window of his room and he soared once again. Gravity almost forgotten, a useless thing, his soul pushed his body until the space before the window no longer had anything to do with the window, but was a space, a space so beautiful, so clear, so completely his that he took it. He conquered it and made it all his own.

● ●

Emma heard all the noise next door and beat on the wall a couple of times, which produced, finally, silence. She went back to her work, her research in children's rights. Emma was drafting a Children's Charter. It was a Magna Charta, a Bill of Rights, a Constitution, and a Declaration of Independence rolled into one.

● ●

Mrs. Sheridan opened the door to Emma's room. Willie was hanging on to her arm, looking in at Emma as though he were at the zoo.

"Emma?"

"Mmm."

"Emma, your father and I are going out to dinner. Martha will make supper for you. Emma?"

"Mmm."

"She don't hear nothing," said Willie.

"She doesn't hear anything," said Mrs. Sheridan.

"That's right," said Willie complacently. "Not a thing."

"Emma?"

"Yes."

"Emma, look at me when I talk to you."

A pair of eyes as glazed as doughnuts moved up to rest near her left earlobe.

"We won't be out late."

"Have a nice time," said a voice lost in 1776.

"She don't hear nothing," said Willie again as Mrs. Sheridan closed the door to her daughter's room.

"Anything," she said absently as she rustled up the hall, the wide, flowing legs of her silk pants suit making

27

a noise that enchanted Willie.

"Beautiful! You look so beautiful!" he said happily, bouncing, skipping, jumping along behind her.

They both admired Mr. Sheridan when he appeared in his tuxedo. "I feel like a panda," he said gruffly.

"You look beautiful!" said Willie.

"Oh, for . . ." Mr. Sheridan was through the door and in the hall, ringing for the elevator.

"Goodbye, Martha, we won't be late," called Mrs. Sheridan. "Goodbye, darling." She bent and kissed Willie.

"Come on," said the bear in the hall.

"Bye, Mommy!" yelled Willie. He closed the door behind them and skipped to the kitchen. "Hi!" he said wildly to Martha.

"Did you wash your hands?"

"Nope."

"Wash."

"Yep." Willie ran down the hall, colliding fiercely with Emma as she floated out of her room.

"Were you listening at my door?" She clutched the front of his shirt.

"To what? The pages turning?" Willie squirmed.

"You were, you little rat, I'll—"

"Emma." Martha stood at the end of the hall. "Stop that and wash your hands. Go into your parents' bathroom. I don't want the two of you at that sink at the same time."

Emma dropped Willie like dirty laundry and stomped down the hall.

Willie stuck out his tongue at her silently, felt himself all over to see if he was maimed and, finding that he was whole, danced to the bathroom.

At dinner they sat opposite each other, with Martha in between.

"Pass the butter," said Emma. Martha took it from Willie and passed it to Emma. There was silence after that.

"Pass the butter," said Willie. Martha took it from Emma and passed it to Willie. More silence.

"Pass the butter," said Emma.

"What is this?" said Martha.

"What?" They both looked up at her in surprise.

"Are you two aware that I have done nothing but pass the butter back and forth for half an hour?"

Willie giggled.

"Why don't you seat us next to each other and put the butter in between?" said Emma humorlessly.

"Because you hit me," said Willie.

"What are you talking about, you little idiot? And what were you doing in your room all afternoon?"

"Practicing leaps."

"Hah! The nigger Nijinsky!" said Emma ferociously.

"Emma!" Martha was appalled. "Emma, that's the worst thing I ever heard in my life. Now you apologize, right this minute!"

"It's better than faggot," said Willie, eating his peas.

"You will leave the table, Emma, if you don't apologize," said Martha.

That did it. Emma had no intention of leaving the table until she finished. "I apologize."

"Sincerely. I want you to mean it."

"Oh, little brother, friend of the white man, I meant you no harm. I would not hurt a nap on your nappy head."

Martha wasn't quite sure what to make of this, so she let it go.

Willie laughed. "Big Chief Loony Lady Lawyer," he crowed.

Emma gave him a murderous look, but kept eating steadily.

"You two are too much," said Martha. "I'm glad my kids don't carry on the way you do. I'd go right out of my mind if they did. Do you want some of this fresh custard I made or do you want ice cream?"

"Both," said Emma.

"Neither," said Willie.

"Now look, you two. You have to lose weight, Emma, and Willie here has to gain. I'm going to give Willie both, and you neither one."

"I'll explode," said Willie helplessly.

Emma regarded Martha with a steady eye. "You can be put in jail, you know, for depriving children of food."

"You look deprived," said Martha.

"Ha ha hee hee." Willie felt hysterical. He hated for people to fight, and particularly Emma. It terrified him. Emma glared at him, then at Martha.

"It's called maltreatment. You could get maybe five years."

"Your mother put you on a diet and you're staying on a diet. You can have one cling peach. Do you want it?"

"Custard," said Emma, trying to seem casual. Actually, she wanted the custard so much, she was trembling.

"One peach. Take it or leave it."

"I'll take it."

The deal completed, Martha put bowls in front of them and started to clean up the kitchen.

Emma ate the peach without thinking, staring at Willie, who dawdled over his custard. He seemed to eat one bite, then fall into a dream. As she watched the custard slide into his mouth, Emma tasted it mentally.

"What are you looking at?" Willie asked uncomfortably. He knew what she was looking at, but he said it hoping to stop her. He was taking his life in his hands, however, and he knew it.

Emma leaned toward him and whispered, "The ugliest little boy I ever saw in my life."

Willie wailed one long cry and burst into terrible tears. He pushed back his chair and ran from the room. Martha turned, said, "What—" and ran after him down the hall.

Emma grabbed the custard, ate it, and put back the

bowl and spoon. Martha came back into the kitchen.

"What did you do to him?"

"Nothing."

"Don't tell me that."

"What?"

"Don't roll those eyes at me. If you've finished, get out of my sight. The way you hurt that child is disgusting to me and I don't like to look at it."

Emma got up and left the room. She thumped with dignity down the hall. There was no sound at all from Willie's room. She closed her heart to the silence, preferring to forget the custard and to return to her usual put-upon feeling. She flipped on the television set as she entered her room, picked up the heavy book she had been reading, and went back to her work, plunking herself down in her armchair, which was so torn, rubbed, and washed out that it looked as though it had fleas.

● ●

Willie lay on his back, staring at the ceiling, fat tears running slowly down his cheeks. He cried silently, not wanting Emma to hear, not wanting to talk to anybody ever again about anything. The television, which he had left on through dinner because he hated coming back into a silent room, was softly going through its tricks. Horatio Selby, M.D., was telling everybody how to live, as usual. Willie watched the complacent white man explain how simple everything was if you just did such and such. He'd never had Emma for a sister—that was clear. He'd never wanted to be a dancer, either.

The thought of this skinny white man as a dancer made Willie laugh. He thought of Dipsey with joy, Dipsey with his neat body moving so good, moving around, just slow and easy. He tried to imagine Dipsey on a stage, but then he had seen a stage only once, when Dipsey had taken him into a theater.

All Willie had seen was a darkened orchestra pit and an enormous empty stage lit by one light, but then he had looked up and his heart had soared with him, up and up, and he had run up onto the stage and looked out into the audience and felt like his pants were falling off. The whole thing did something to him and he couldn't say what it was, but the question of living with Emma became unimportant. Emma became, in fact, boring. Emma, next to whatever was in that place and the life that went on there and the way it all felt to him, became a heavy old frump, meaningless.

The knock surprised him, and Emma's face, when he opened the door, even more. He had become caught up in Dr. Selby's easiness, lulled into dreams of the stage and the life that went with it, a life that meant to him, essentially, a life without Emma.

"I'm sorry."

"What?" He looked genuinely puzzled, but memory pushed at him. "Oh." He stared at her. To say the wrong thing at this moment promised a worse horror.

"I shouldn't have said that. I'm sorry."

"Okay." He laughed at her. "I know I'm not ugly."

A look of fury came over her face, and, too late, he knew he had said the wrong thing. Why could he never say anything right to her? She turned on her heel. He closed the door.

She marched into the bathroom. "Little rat," she muttered. She sat on the john with a thud. "Little creepo rat. Hates me. Laughs at me. Thinks he's beautiful. An entire Sidney Poitier."

She looked across to the mirror on the door, at the vision of herself on the john. "Blech," she said loudly.

Before she flushed, she examined her productions with earnest horror. "I guess his have ribbons on them," she said as she flushed enthusiastically. She laughed as she washed her hands. She had a silent laugh. Her shoulders shook, but no noise came out.

She gave herself a particularly murderous look in the mirror. "Burn, baby, burn," she said ominously. Laughing silently again, she watched herself laugh silently. Suddenly she thought of the ceiling of the bathroom gone, as in a dollhouse, and people looking in on her, in there wagging her head and laughing at herself in the mirror.

"Into the booby hatch, right?" she yelled up to the ceiling. The flat bathroom light looked back at her blankly.

She opened the door, let it crash behind her against the sink, and marched down the hall. There was something to look up, she remembered, something that had to do with the legal rights of, for instance, brothers, little brothers. She could hear Willie in his room, dancing wildly.

When she got to her room, there was a program on television that made her drop everything and watch. Gloria Steinem was interviewing some women prominent in the women's liberation movement. One of the women was a lawyer.

Wow. The woman said that her father had been a lawyer and that he hadn't wanted her to be a lawyer and that he had, in fact, taken her to court when she was seven years old for stealing a dime from her mother's purse. The judge had told her father he was crazy to bring a kid into court like that and ought to have his head examined.

Emma nodded sagely. The woman said that it hadn't changed the way her father was, even having a *judge* say something to him hadn't done a damned thing. Emma nodded again, feeling friendly. She watched Gloria Steinem's face as she talked and wished that she looked like her. There was one black woman on the panel. She was a producer in the theater. Emma dismissed her, after taking in her clothes, as not as serious as the other people. What the hell was the theater compared to the Law and other important things that got changes made in this world? What was the difference between the theater and singing and dancing on the levee? Fools. Running for Congress, now that meant something. They were talking about male mentality, about it causing wars. Wars? They ought to have a talk with Willie the Flit. He couldn't even rouse a good battle, never mind a war. Emma thought they were all wrong. The trouble with men was that they were butterfly-headed, not dangerous, just silly; then, suddenly, she thought of her father. She had never thought of her father as a man before. She thought of him rather like one thinks of Boulder Dam. He was something to scale or go over in a barrel.

In thinking of her father, she changed the way she listened. Yes. Was this thing, this male chauvinism they were talking about, what made him treat her that way? Is that why he ignored what she said, squirmed around, and looked embarrassed? Although he looked embarrassed when he looked at Willie, too. But then, who wouldn't look embarrassed looking at Willie? That was understandable, but what was embarrassing when she, Emma, asked a perfectly reasonable question? Why did their mother seem proud of them both in that ineffectual way, and their father seem to hate them both?

Jealous. They were saying that men were jealous and didn't want competition. Jealous? Her father jealous of her?

Wouldn't that be nice!

Wasn't that the kind of thing he indicated last night when he said to her mother that he thought Emma would get a better grade on the bar exam than he did?

Okay. It was clear what to do then, just get a better grade on the bar exam than he did.

But who would get her in to take the bar exam? Eleven years old. Had anybody ever taken the exam at eleven? Here was something to look up tonight in his law books before he got home. If anybody ever had, even at twelve, then she would write a letter to the Bar Association. Naturally, it would help to have him back her up, but it was not impossible to do without him.

● ●

Getting up quickly, she went into her father's study. She began to look through the law books, but was soon frustrated because, in truth, she did not know where to look. She expected to find a book which said something like "Requirements for Passing the State Bar Exam" on the cover, and when she didn't, she wandered among the books like a dog lost in the snow, turning in circles and walking up and down, then turning again.

She sat down at the desk and went into a trance of pretending. She pretended to pick up the phone and rail at her secretary. "Where are those contracts? What do you mean, you don't have them? Your baby lost one of its arms? What does that mean, Miss Googler? Be more specific if you can. That is, which arm, and where did she lose it? In Bloomingdale's? So? I don't see that that's any reason for not getting back from the hospital in time to type those contracts. Get them in here on my desk in fifteen minutes . . . What's that? Each contract is fifty to one hundred pages long? So what, Miss Googler? You'll never think like a man until you get rid of all this emotional nit-picking. Fifteen minutes. Is that clear?"

She pretended to bang the phone down, then leaned back in the swivel chair, on her face an expression of sublime, besotted joy.

Bored with that, she began to look through the papers on her father's desk. One stack was topped by a note which said "Old Cases—Put in Dead File." Obviously these were cases he had tried before becoming an assistant district attorney. Under the note was a small book with Bible-thin pages entitled *Merck Manual*.

Emma opened it up. It was a medical book. As she flipped through, reading parts of entries, she began to marvel at it. It seemed to be a book you could take into the jungles of Africa. You could stay for years curing people right and left without even being a doctor. It even had directions for operating. You'd have to take along a dictionary, of course, for half the words were gibberish.

Emma looked up menstruation, which was new to her, an addition to her life activities which she could not be said to have welcomed.

The index referred her to *Menstruation, disorders of,* and the first one on the list was *Amenorrhea,* under which it said *Absence of menstruation.*

"Wow!" Emma spoke loudly to the room. "How can I get that?"

She read on: Physiologic amenorrhea occurs before the menarche [Who is he? the King? the King of the Period?], after menopause [The pause that men take?], during pregnancy and lactation [I have so many lacks that now I have a severe case of lactation?].

She decided she'd better look up a few words, but first, it occurred to her to wonder why this book was on her father's desk.

She rummaged around. It had been lying neatly on a stack of papers.

In this stack she found the legal pad on which her father had sketched out his brief. She began to read, picking through his handwriting as through a dark closet.

From what she could gather, her father had been the attorney for a man who had had an operation during which the surgeon had been forgetful. He had left inside the man's stomach a large rubber glove, a pair of forceps, and a small sponge.

The man had, needless to say, become uncomfortable and had submitted to another operation at another hospital, wherein the lost objects were found and reported. The man had retained Emma's father as attorney and was suing the first hospital and the doctor who had so carelessly misplaced his tools.

Emma felt slightly ill. She looked at the medical book and saw that there was a piece of paper marking a place. Turning to that place, she read what her father had evidently been reading, a passage entitled *Obstruction,* and felt even worse.

It became important to see if the man operated on was a black man. He was.

"Typical," Emma said aloud. "If it had been a black woman, they would have left fourteen scalpels and a coat hanger inside."

She put everything back into the stack neatly and leaned back into the chair.

Musing, she reviewed things she had heard her father say about doctors. Sifting through various comments, she realized that even though there had been a lot of grumbling, her father seemed to have a grudging respect. Even when the doctor was a woman?

Yes! She remembered now. A friend of her mother's was a doctor. She had come to visit a couple of times. Yes! Her father had seemed afraid of this woman.

Emma felt a surge of greatness. Oh, to make her father afraid. What a feeling that would be. Not only to impress him but to have him actually afraid of her, Emma!

She sat up abruptly and grabbed the medical book. Deciding that there was something bothering her about the small mole on her left ear which had been there since birth, she looked up moles in the index. She found: Nevi (Moles, Birthmarks). Moles vary in color from yellow-brown to black. [Just like us darkies, thought Emma.] They may be small or large, flat or raised, smooth, hairy [hairy!] or verrucous [what?], and have a broad or pedunculated base. [I'm going to tell Willie he has a pedunculated base.]

Emma stopped reading. She went off into a dream. She was in medical school. The men made fun of her, but she persisted. She was a drudge about her studies, she made all A's. She was then a resident. Finally, she was a doctor. She sat behind her white desk, in her white office, in a white lab coat. She pushed the buzzer for her secretary to send in her first patient, her very first patient. The door opened and in walked her father.

"Yes, what can I do for you?" (Emma, well-known and respected young New York doctor.)

"Doctor, it's this enormous mole—"

"Ah, yes, no doubt verrucous"—nods head wisely— "and probably having a pedunculated base. Take off your clothes."

"What in hell are you talking about?"

Too late, Emma realized that reality was presenting itself to her in the form of her real father standing in his real doorway to his real office after she, in his real swivel chair, had just said to him, "Take off your clothes," like an ass.

"Hi, Dad." She jumped up and started for the door

like a runaway horse. Only casualness could save her now, casualness and quickness—the quick and the dead.

"Oh, no, you don't! What did that mean?"

She wasn't quick enough, so she wished she were dead.

"Sir?" All innocence now. Try to make him think he's nuts. Last-ditch-stand time.

"What were you doing in here?"

"Sir?"

"What did you mean by saying to me, 'Take off your clothes'?"

"Sir?"

A certain stillness in her father signified the change in him that she feared the most, the switch from father to prosecuting attorney.

His eyes became darker, flatter, colder. "You stated as I entered the room, stated clearly, 'Take off your clothes,' did you not?"

"I did." Hopeless.

"To what purpose did you state this?"

"I was a doctor." No hope except for truth.

"Make yourself clear." Was there a hint, the lightest touch of a feather brush of fear in his eyes?

"I was pretending I was a doctor."

His grip on her arm relaxed. He swung from district attorney back into father quicker than Wolf Man. He smiled.

"Daydreaming?"

"Yes." What a baby thought, what a baby word, daydreams; but it worked. It got her off the hook, and to-day the hook hurt more than most days.

"I'm thinking of becoming a doctor." She said it flatly because she couldn't help herself. Something inside her said it when she had planned to say nothing.

"Oh?" Touch of the feather again, the white feather? He had been moving toward his desk and now he looked back at her, a large, thickset black man with a weary face. "I forgot some papers," he said, opening a drawer.

"Yes." She said it too loudly. Even more loudly she said, "I'm *going* to be a doctor!" She looked him hard in the eyes and went out, slamming the door in his face.

On the way to her room, her knees shaking from delayed fear, she wondered at her own courage and wondered even more why the whole thing had taken courage and wondered even more than that at what in the world she was doing or saying. She didn't want to be a doctor. Blech. Touch people. Ick.

She wanted to change. She opened the door to her room. She relaxed, seeing the familiar mess. She wanted to change, but there must be some other way.

● ●

The next night, Emma sat contemplating the infinite boredom of family dinners. Martha was serving Mrs. Sheridan the green beans. Mr. Sheridan was cutting his steak left-handed in that curious roundabout way of his. Willie was pushing his food around, trying to hide it under his knife, separating it to make his plate look empty when, in reality, he had eaten nothing.

For a moment it seemed to Emma they were caught in a time tunnel. She saw them reeling through space, Willie pushing his food, her father cutting, her mother taking green beans, and herself looking sullenly at them, all of it happening endlessly, never going forward, never going back, just hurtling on forever through parting stars.

"No, thank you," said Willie to Martha.

"Finish the beans on your plate," said Mrs. Sheridan.

"Some dancer you'll be," said Martha. "If you don't eat, you'll be too weak to stand up, let alone dance."

"He's outgrown that, anyway," said Mr. Sheridan, taking an enormous second helping of beans. "People outgrow things, don't they? Isn't that right, Willie?"

Willie kept pushing, looking down and saying nothing.

"How was it downtown today, dear?" Mrs. Sheridan hurried to cover Willie's silence.

The talk droned on over Emma's head as she thought about Willie. Rotten little weasel—his mother protecting him all the time. Doesn't have the guts God gave a banana peel.

"Dad?" Willie looked at his father.

"Don't interrupt," said his father. He was getting to

the best part of his story, the part where he won the case.

"Dad, I want to go away to summer stock."

"You want to what?"

"Go away to summer stock." Willie seemed to be holding his breath.

"What's the kid talking about?" Mr. Sheridan turned helplessly to his wife.

"Summer theater. He wants to try being a dancer for one summer." Mrs. Sheridan looked as if she'd swallowed a fork. "Dipsey knows a theater that's doing *Oliver* this summer and they need a lot of children for that."

"Dipsey? What's that no-count got to do with this?"

"Dipsey's a great dancer!" Willie said excitedly. "He's not no-count. He works all the time. He's teaching me and he says I'm good enough right now to work with him!"

"Out of the question." Mr. Sheridan returned to his food.

"He'd be there with me, Dad. I could make money!"

"Don't even think about it."

"He says I could make two or three hundred dollars."

"I don't want to hear any more about it."

"I'd give you the money, Dad."

Mr. Sheridan put down his fork. He looked right into Willie's eyes.

"He doesn't mean anything bad, William."

Mr. Sheridan put his napkin on the table. He leaned back, staring at Willie as though he'd never seen him before. "Just what kind of a guy do you think I am? Look at me, son. What kind of a man you think your father is? You think I'd send you out to work at seven years old and *take the money?*"

"No, sir." Willie was examining his belt buckle.

"You think I'd send a child out to work so I could live off him? You don't think much of me, do you?"

"William, he's not thinking anything like that."

"I think it's time we *found out* what he's thinking. He's making plans right and left and—"

Mr. Sheridan was interrupted by Martha's entrance. She passed hot rolls and they all shut up while she was in the room. This always irritated Emma. Martha probably heard every word in the kitchen, so why couldn't they just keep talking? They sat, instead, in phony silence, each in turn saying "No, thank you," until it was Emma's turn and she took three. Nobody noticed.

"I think what Willie wants to do in life should be given some consideration," said Mrs. Sheridan gently.

Willie's eyes were wild with hope.

"Wants to do in life? That's absurd. He's seven years old." Mr. Sheridan turned to Willie. "You want to work? If you want to work, why don't you sell newspapers?"

"Or swimming pools," said Emma.

Everyone looked at her in astonishment. "There's a

lot of money to be made selling pools. I read it in the Sunday paper."

"Don't talk with your mouth full," said Mrs. Sheridan absently. They all turned away again. She ate another roll.

"Just what is it you want to do?" asked Mr. Sheridan.

"I want to be a dancer." Willie was so quiet and scared they could hardly hear him.

"Son." Mr. Sheridan pushed back his chair, crossed his legs, and lit a cigar. "I want to tell you something and I want you to listen. There are many jobs in this world and some are good, decent jobs for good, decent men to have. Others are jobs that aren't even to be thought about. Now, these people who spend their lives running around a stage are just trash. You don't want to be trash, do you?"

Mrs. Sheridan looked outraged. "William! My father wasn't—"

"I'm not talking about your father. Your father came along there in the Depression where a black man couldn't get a decent job. Singing and dancing were all they let him do. Everything's entirely different now. What do you think I work myself to death for? My kid's got every chance in the world. He doesn't have to run around dancing, making a fool of himself, laughing and scratching to make honkies laugh. He's got the whole world ahead of him. He's going to a private school. He's going to college. He doesn't *need* to do the kinds of things your father did."

"But he wants to. He's like my father. He's just like Dipsey when Dipsey was small. Don't you think that what he wants to do ought to be given some consideration?"

"He's seven years old, woman. He doesn't know his left ear from his right. What does what *he* want got to do with it? Four years ago he wanted to be a rabbit."

"That's different!" Willie looked angry. "I know now what I want. And I'm going to get it, too!"

"You shut up, Willie. You don't talk like that to your father, not now, not ever, do you talk to me like that. You understand? You've got other people to consider besides yourself. You've got to think of all the people who have bled and died so other people don't look at you and see nothing but a minstrel show. You want to take all that and throw it in their faces and say, 'Look at me, yassur, boss, you right, I ain't good for nothing but singing and dancing and picking cotton'?"

"William, really!"

"I think that's true," said Emma. Nobody had asked her and nobody paid any attention to her. She ate another roll.

"I don't care about them!" Willie jumped up. "I only care about one thing." He started running. "I'm going to do it, too!" His voice came back at them from down the hall.

Mr. Sheridan blew a large puff of smoke. His big face looked more like a walrus than ever.

"He doesn't know anything about all that." Mrs. Sheridan was looking at her husband with something like pity.

"How much that Dipsey been coming round here?"

"If you're finished, Emma, you may be excused." Mrs. Sheridan smiled at Emma.

"There's chocolate mousse," said Emma.

"He coming round here every day?" Mr. Sheridan blew more smoke.

"Of course not," said Mrs. Sheridan. "He's given Willie a few lessons, that's all. He's just trying to help."

"Well, tell him to stop coming round." More smoke.

"I can't do that. It would break Willie's heart."

"He's giving the child ideas. Can't you see that? We don't need him round here filling the kid full of fancy thoughts." Mr. Sheridan was puffing so hard there were clouds of smoke all over the dining room.

"Look, William. I can see your point about summer stock. I think he's too young for that too, but I don't see why he has to cut out dancing altogether, and I don't agree with you about people in show business being trash. I should think you'd think about my father being in show business for forty years before you say anything like that."

"You do, huh." Mr. Sheridan rolled his cigar in his mouth in a way that made Emma think of gangster movies. "Well, I'll tell you something, woman. This is my son I'm talking to. Don't you think a man knows a little bit more about what to say to his son than you do? Seeing as how I'm a man and he's going to be a man? I know what's right for my son, so don't you worry your head about this." He got up and moved toward the living room.

"Don't you want any dessert?"

"No. I'll take my coffee in the living room."

They heard the rustle of the newspaper as he unfolded it. Martha came in and put the chocolate mousse in front of Mrs. Sheridan. "Only two of us, I guess, Martha. You might take this to Willie and see if he'll eat a little." She handed a bowl to Martha, who took it down the hall to Willie's room.

Emma ate silently, watching her mother out of the corner of her eye.

Mrs. Sheridan seemed nervous, fluttery, and not altogether herself. She saw Emma looking at her.

"How was school today, dear?"

"What do you feel about women's liberation?" Emma fired at her.

Mrs. Sheridan looked amused. "As you know, I do volunteer work for the day-care center."

"That doesn't answer my question."

"It was a rather general question. What is it you want to know?"

"Are you going to let Dad push you around like that, or are you going to fight?"

"Fight?" Mrs. Sheridan looked surprised.

"Fight for what you believe in."

"And what is that?"

"You believe Willie ought to go to summer stock?"

"No. I don't. He's too young."

"But you believe he ought to keep on dancing?"

"Yes." Mrs. Sheridan sounded tentative, as though she were listening to herself. "Yes, I think . . . I don't see anything wrong with dancing."

"Well, *he* sure does." Emma helped herself to more mousse.

"Yes, that's true." Mrs. Sheridan sounded far away.

"Well, then. You going to fight or not?"

"I don't know," said Mrs. Sheridan.

"While you're at it, I'd like to be a lawyer and he doesn't like that either."

Mrs. Sheridan looked at Emma and burst out laughing. "You'll get over that, dear."

"Oh, swell," said Emma.

Mrs. Sheridan kept on laughing. Emma kept on eating. She finished off her chocolate mousse. She scraped the bowl. She sat back and looked at her mother, who was now sitting quietly, with an amused expression.

"You think I'm funny?"

"What, dear?"

"Am I funny?"

Mrs. Sheridan looked at Emma. She saw a round face trying to look brave, expecting the worst and on the verge of tears. "No, dear, of course not. Where did you ever get that idea?"

"You laughed."

"Did I, dear? Well, yes, I guess I did. It was funny."

"What's funny about being a lawyer?"

"It's not that being a lawyer is funny. It's the idea of you as a lawyer. Why in the world would you want to do that?"

"You think I'm too stupid?" Emma found she was holding her breath.

"I just can't imagine why you'd want to do that."

"You do think I'm stupid."

"Of course you're not stupid. You get straight A's in school. It's the *life* of a lawyer. I think you're too young to realize that the life of a lawyer is very rough. If you knew more about it, I don't think you'd choose it. I don't think you'd be thinking about it at all."

"What would I choose?" Emma began to feel crafty. She felt as though she had her mother on a witness stand.

"I think you'd choose marrying a man you loved, marrying a lawyer perhaps, and raising two lovely children—"

"I'd put a bullet through my head before I'd marry a lawyer."

"—but I can't see you doing what a lawyer has to do,

hanging around a hot courthouse, interviewing a lot of criminals. Sometimes it's even dangerous."

"I don't even want to get married, much less have children."

"Of course you do. You're only eleven. You don't know what you want yet."

"I know exactly what I want." Emma was in control now. "And I know what you want. You want me to be you! You want me to be exactly like you." She felt triumphant. The secret was out.

"Oh, no, dear. I know you're not like me." There was sarcasm in her mother's voice. "I know you've had a totally different life."

Emma began to feel uncomfortable, as though she were losing in some mysterious way. She turned into a prosecuting attorney. "You said, did you not, that I should marry a lawyer and have two lovely children. That's what you said!"

"Your life is totally unlike mine. Look at the advantages you've had, a nice home, a private school, your mother and father with you every evening. I played backstage in a dressing room and slept in rotten hotels with cockroaches. My mother was dead, and my father half drunk all the time. I had to take care of Dipsey, raise him when I wasn't even raised myself. Oh, no, I see your life is different!"

Emma sat motionless, dumbfounded by guilt. Here she was, with all the things her mother never had. Why wasn't she happy? Because she was a miserable spoiled brat who did nothing but make her mother unhappy. She resolved to change.

"I'm sorry, Mother." She felt like a big fat nerd. She had never hated herself so much as at this moment.

"Sorry? What have *you* got to be sorry about?" Her mother laughed again. The laugh cut through Emma's soul. She, Emma, was obviously laughable, a clown, a buffoon, an idiot, with her ideas about being a lawyer. Who would ever hire a fat black mess to defend them?

She had a vision of herself in a large, flowered dress and a straw hat, like somebody out of a cotton field, addressing the court.

"Your honor, may it please the court—"

"Who is that woman? Get that woman out of here. Clear the court of these people not connected with the trial." Bang bang bang of the gavel.

"Your honor, I am the attorney for the defense"—saying this over and over as two strong bailiffs dragged her from the courtroom. Looking across at the prosecutor, who was, out of the two hundred assistant district attorneys of the borough of Manhattan, none other than her father, she saw that he was not recognizing her because to do so would be to call shame upon himself. He was laughing along with everyone else at the fat lady being dragged out of court.

"You have nothing to be sorry about." How long had her mother been talking? "You have a good life. Your father has worked hard to give us all a good life. You have everything to look forward to and nothing to worry about."

"Can I finish the chocolate mousse?" There was no point in dieting now.

"*May* I," said Mrs. Sheridan, looking for the first time at the big bowl. "Goodness, Emma, you've almost eaten the entire thing. No, you may not, we must leave some for Martha. And, honey, you *must* diet. You don't want to grow up to be a big fat woman, do you?"

What else? thought Emma as she got up and walked staunchly to her room.

That night on television there was a program on children's rights. Emma became involved as never before. She took down a phone number, given out by a sixteen-year-old physics genius in spectacles. She hid the number in the pocket of her book bag.

● ●

Spring came through the window of the schoolroom and hit Willie on the head. He could hear the traffic down below, but the air that came in was sweet, a lost, bright sweetness that made him ache.

The next time he saw the teacher pause, he raised his hand to be excused.

Once in the hall, he ran. If he didn't get to the phone fast, he'd never have time before the next class.

The phone booth was right across from the principal's office. He sidled in and closed the door quietly.

He dialed the number. It rang four times before Dipsey answered.

"Dipsey?"

"Whoof."

"Dipsey, it's Willie!"

"Aw, come on, kid, I told you not to call me before noon on Fridays. You know I work at the club on Thursdays."

"I had to. I'm sorry. I figured if I waited you'd go out soon as you woke up."

"That's what my agent always says." Dipsey gave a big yawn. "What's up, anyway?"

"Dipsey, I got to go."

"Hey, kid, you wake me up in the middle of the night to tell me you got to hang up the phone?"

"No, I mean, I got to go to summer stock."

"Not today, you don't have to go. Whyn't you and me talk about that at some reasonable hour, like, say, three in the afternoon?"

"Dipsey, this is serious. I got to do it."

There was a pause. "I don't know, kid."

"I got to. I just got to!"

"I don't know what we're going to do about this, kid. Your daddy don't like the idea and he can get pretty stuffy when he don't like something."

"You got to listen to me. I'm going to kill myself if I don't go!"

"Hold it, kid, now wait a minute. Listen, let me get a cup of coffee. I'm not even awake. I'm hearing things."

"I mean it. There's nothing else I want in the whole world. I ain't any good at anything else, Dipsey." Willie felt his voice breaking. What a time to turn into a crybaby. He bit his lip. "I got to. I just got to do this."

"Take it easy, kid. Where are you, anyway?"

"School."

"What time you get out of school?"

"Three o'clock, but I can't come over then because I'm supposed to be home right after school. Can't I come over now, Dipsey? Please, can't I?"

"Listen, kid, seeing me ain't going to do anything. What good is—"

"Please, Dipsey, please, just let me come over."

There was another, longer pause.

"Okay, kid. I may be doing the wrong thing, but I don't know how to say no when you sound like that. You know how to get here?"

"Sure. I'll be right over."

Willie forgot to say goodbye. He hung up and ran out of the booth and down the hall.

The bell was ringing loudly. People were coming out of all the doors.

Willie ran, got his books, ran down the three flights

of steps, jumped past the monitor when his back was turned, then out the door and onto Park Avenue.

He ran around the corner, hoping that no teacher was looking out the window, ran across Madison, got to Fifth, and hopped on the bus just as the doors were closing.

He felt that everybody on the bus was looking at him in his blue blazer with his book bag, wondering what he was doing out of school at eleven-thirty.

A fat, crazy-looking white man in a purple tie and a green hat kept looking him up and down as though he were a tiger escaped from the zoo. Maybe he was a cop, but he didn't look like a cop. He just looked like a crazy person. The man rolled his eyes three times, tapped his foot three times, then went back to looking Willie up and down. He wasn't any cop. Willie moved away from him.

He got off at Sixtieth and Fifth, ran toward the Plaza Hotel. People were everywhere. The spring air was bringing them out. The sun was beginning to be hot. People were joking and laughing. The sweet air touched Willie's face as he ran, making him glad, making him not care what happened when he got to Dipsey's. He felt the air and he knew it would be all right. Everything would always be all right. "Yeh," he yelled at the doorman of the Plaza, for no reason at all. The doorman laughed and waved at him.

He ran around the corner, past a garage, and there he was at Dipsey's building.

Willie loved this building. It seemed right in the middle of everything. And there was a movie right across the street, where Dipsey could go any time he wanted!

He punched the bell that said Dipsey Bates. The buzzer sounded back. He pushed the door and went to the elevator, which was standing open.

Dipsey lived on the fifth floor. Willie punched the button and started dancing.

He danced all over the elevator, singing a song he made up on the spot.

"Five is the number, five is the place, give me five and I'll win the race."

He did the fastest time step he could do. "Five is lucky, I am too. Look at this, this a soft shoe."

He did a soft shoe. Then, when the door opened, he did a shuffle-off-to-Buffalo right down the hall to Dipsey's door.

He pushed the buzzer. Dancing always made him so happy that for a moment he forgot why he was there.

He was tapping away when Dipsey opened the door.

"Well, now, this here don't look a bit like somebody going to kill himself."

Willie stopped, surprised.

"Hey, Willie Boy!" Dipsey gave him a big hug. "Come on in here. And a one and a two!"

Dipsey started dancing with him, so they both came into the apartment dancing. He was tapping fast and Dipsey was tapping back at him.

Willie stopped abruptly when he saw someone else in the apartment. A white man in a black turtleneck sweater sat with his back to the window. The sun poured in past him, so that his face was in the dark and Willie couldn't make out his features.

Dipsey led him across the room. "This is Mr. Diamond, Willie."

"Call me Pete." The man didn't move, but Willie could see his face now, could see he was smiling.

"Tell you what, Willie Boy. I'm going to give you a lesson. Okay?"

"Sure!" Willie looked over at the man named Pete.

"Never mind him. Come on, Willie, take off your coat. Let's go!"

Dipsey already had the record started. Before Willie got his jacket off, he could see Dipsey all over the place. The music was ragtime, slow and fast at the same time.

"Come on!" said Dipsey. "This here's the 'Fig Leaf Rag.' That's Scott Joplin's music. You won't hear any better than that! That's right, Willie, nice and easy, now here we go, gentle like, first we give it to them, then we take it back, that's it, don't let them know your secrets, let them guess, that's it, boy, let's go now, hit it, let 'em have it, let 'em have it good!"

Willie took off, doing just what Dipsey was doing. It was wild. He forgot anybody was in the room at all.

"That's it, build, gently, build and build, and now, break, break, Willie. Hit it!"

The record that came on next was so fast that Willie thought he would lose his mind. He and Dipsey pounded the floor and got lost completely in the sound. It went on and on, faster and faster. Willie had never felt anything like it. He felt his soul would bust in two and his head fly right out the window, but he kept following Dipsey and doing just exactly what Dipsey was doing, in and out of time steps and breaks and shuffles and cakewalks.

"Now we going to slow down, here we go slower down to the end of the music. That's right, Willie Boy, nice and slow like syrup pouring, easy and smooth and out. Stop."

Willie managed to stop at exactly the moment Dipsey did, and he felt prouder than he ever had in his life.

Pete applauded. Willie had forgotten all about him.

Pete winked at him. "You pretty good, kid."

"Okay, Willie, go get yourself a soda in the icebox. Bring me a glass of water while you're out there."

Willie ran to the kitchen. As he got the soda out, he could hear Dipsey talking.

"What do you think, Pete?"

"I think he's terrific, but you know how it is, Dipsey.

We got to have the director, the producer, the writers. I'm just the press agent. I don't have anything to say, you know that."

"Yeah, but what do you think?"

"I think he's great. What do you want from me? You know this business."

"Yeah, even the janitor gives notes."

"Right, and if the director, God forbid, has a nephew, I can see him now, ten years old, fat and pimply, with a case of the cutes, not able to dance his way out of a bag, that's the one that will get the part."

Dipsey took the water as though Willie were a midget waiter, not noticing him at all.

"They want *me*, don't they?" Dipsey took a big gulp of water.

"Sure. You're signed, aren't you? I know they talked to your agent. You're set."

"Well, how about they want me they got to take Willie here?"

"Aw, come off it, Dipsey. You're kidding! You wouldn't pull that, would you? Besides, this is a good spot for you. This one's on Broadway! You can't afford to do that to yourself. I mean, the kid's good, but—I think that would be stupid. The kid's got a lot of years ahead of him. If he doesn't make this, there'll be a lot of other things for him, but what about you? How many parts come along for you? This is tailor-made for you. You'd be an idiot not to do it. I wouldn't even risk it by suggesting such a thing."

"I'm not saying I would, I'm not saying I wouldn't. I just wondered what you thought."

"Well, that's what I think. I think your agent would agree with me. I got to go."

Pete got up. He put his hand on Willie's head. "Thanks for the show, kid. Someday you're going to knock 'em dead."

Willie moved away. He hated having his head touched. He also hated the way this guy was sounding. He made everything sound hard, impossible even. What seemed simple before, spending the summer with Dipsey and dancing, now sounded like the hardest thing in the world. He went over and sat by the window while they said goodbye at the door.

Dipsey came back. "I know. It ain't all sugar candy." He walked away a little. "I'll tell you something, Willie, don't nobody ever hand you a dream. You've got to fight for a dream, and you've got to keep on fighting way after you have any strength. You got to get more strength, and pick yourself up again, and you got to go on. It's the only way." He did a fast, happy step. "Now come on, let's get you ready for this audition!"

● ●

At the same moment Willie went into the phone booth, Emma went into the phone booth at her school.

"Hello?"

"Hello? Is this Harrison Carter?"

"Yes, who is this?"

"Are you the Harrison Carter that's good in physics and that was on TV last night?"

"Yes. Who is this?"

"Do you really believe all those things you said last night?"

"Listen, if you're another one of those creeps calling about the show, let me tell you that you're not very original. Everybody and his dog has called me to tell me I'm un-American, I ought to be shot, why don't I cut my hair—"

"Wait a minute! I liked the show!"

"Oh?" Harrison Carter paused. He sounded suspicious.

"I thought it was great. I want to come to a meeting."

"You do? What's your name?"

"Emma Sheridan. I'm eleven."

"How do you do. You want to join us?"

"Yes. What do I do?"

"Where do you live?"

"Seventy-ninth and East End."

"Then you'd be in the Anne Frank Brigade. They meet on Eighty-first Street. You want the address?"

"Is that just for girls?"

"No. We don't have segregated brigades. Each one is named after a famous victim, real or literary, like Oliver

Twist or Peter Jensen."

"Who's Peter Jensen?"

"He was killed at Watts. His mother'd sent him out to the bakery and he was shot down."

"Wow." Emma paused. "What do these brigades do?"

"See, we've organized ourselves into the Children's Army, which is made up of brigades decided by neighborhood because, as you know, our people have trouble getting across town alone without thousands of questions from parents, but they can go around the block. This is all Top Secret, by the way. You're not to tell anyone, nor are you to recognize other members on the street if you or they are with a parent. Hey, you want to come to the rally this afternoon? All the brigades will be there, so you'll meet everybody."

"What time?"

"Four p.m. in a warehouse not far from you, at Seventy-ninth and the river. You go around the back and there's a door. There's a very small sign on the door, about as large as a stamp, and the sign says HERE. Everybody has to bring a box of cookies."

"Cookies?"

"Cookies. We'll explain later."

"What kind of cookies?"

"Any kind."

"What do I wear?"

"Anything."

"Is there anything else I have to know?"

"No. You'll find out everything when you're there. I look forward to meeting you in person."

"I'm large and I'm black," said Emma hurriedly.

"You saw what I look like, a flamingo with acne."

"Nobody's perfect," said Emma. "I'll be there."

"Right. Glad to have you with us."

Emma got out of the phone booth as though she were in Prague, had on a trench coat, and were being followed by Peter Lorre. She sped down the hall and into her English class, which seemed now, although she had always liked it before, like so much child's play, sandbox time.

When school let out, she ran to the delicatessen on the corner. The crippled man who owned it was sitting on a stool. His hard-working wife was scrubbing as usual. Emma went to the cookie section. She pondered the boxes. Personally she preferred Mallomars, but what did revolutionaries eat? It would be awful to appear holding some kind of reactionary cookie that everyone had stopped eating years ago, like those pink puffs there looking a bit like Zsa Zsa Gabor, obviously capitalist cookies.

Other kids began to come in after school. Emma stood pondering, pushed here and there as kids crowded through the small space left between Emma's body and the wall.

Chocolate grahams looked stodgy, little Wall Street men all lined up. European cookies? The powdered-sugar German ones would never do, no sir, not in the Anne Frank Brigade. French? Too decadent, possibly, too reminiscent of "Let them eat cake." Let them eat cookies.

Emma burst out laughing at the thought. She laughed silently, however, so all anyone saw was her huge body rocking to and fro in front of the cookie section.

An arm reached in front of her for a box of cookies. The idea hit Emma that any one of these kids in the deli could belong to the Children's Army and that here she was, and would be forever remembered, laughing herself to death in front of the cookie section.

She grabbed a box of Mallomars. Two? Should she take two boxes? Had he said bring a *box* of cookies, or had he said bring *cookies?* Better not take two, they might think she was some rich snot, better to be poor than rich in this group. She took the box up to the counter and paid for it.

A girl in a green raincoat holding a box of cookies eyed her, then quickly looked away. Aha! thought Emma.

She left the store. On the way to Seventy-ninth, she opened the cookies absentmindedly as she thought about the curious trait in her character which always made her angry at whatever it was she was about to commit herself to. She could do it even about small things—for instance, choosing a book in the library. If she started to like the book very much, she would suddenly get suspicious and say all sorts of terrible things to herself about the book, such as it's probably a bore, who would read that anyway and I never really liked the cover, what am I standing here holding it in my hand for? She would put the book back on the shelf and then take it out again. This indecision didn't always plague her. If she just went into the library and picked up a book without thinking about it very much, there was no problem. It was when she suddenly wanted to read that book more than anything else in the world.

So it was today. The idea that there was a group of people intent on fighting all the injustice she saw around her, a group to which she could actually belong (that is, she was a child and this was a children's army, so nobody could say she couldn't belong), and not only that, the idea of a group which was aware of all the things she was aware of, the unfairness of being a child, the blindness of parents, how hard it all was, the idea that this seemed to be a perfect group for her, sent chills through her and at the same time made her balk, made her wonder if she was deluding herself and this was just a bunch of crazies. If she got down there and they were all sitting around making bombs, or even spitballs, she would leave and she would tell them why she was leaving too. She, Emancipation Sheridan, was a pacifist. She didn't believe in doing all the same stupid things that adults did. There had to be a better way.

If, furthermore, they were all sitting around in that

warehouse eating cookies and serving tea like a bunch of Mad Hatters and this was a social thing, where you met all the right people, she would leave too, because they would be an impossibly deluded bunch.

She crossed East End Avenue, putting a cookie into her mouth.

If, on the other hand, they really were going to accomplish something, if they really would stick behind each kid and make it easier somehow to get through this business called childhood, and if they really were trying to do something to make life better for children, like that guy Harrison Carter had said on TV, then she would join them.

She saw a trash basket and threw the cookie box. As she watched her arm throw the box, she realized what she had done. She stood, dumbfounded, looking at the empty box lying in the bottom of the basket. She'd eaten every cookie! How could anybody be so stupid? How in the world could anybody be so incredibly dumb as to do such a thing? She looked around to see if anyone had seen her.

God forbid. Here came three girls from her school, all carrying boxes of cookies.

Emma turned her back on them. She pretended to be examining the river. They were laughing and talking to each other. She didn't know them well, because she didn't know anyone well. She had been the only black girl in her class for as long as she could remember. She got smiled at a lot, too much, and people made a point of asking her to eat lunch with them. She would sit down and eat with them, but then she would have eaten lunch if George Wallace had asked her. She never wanted to talk while she was eating, and she never had anything to say to these girls anyway. She had had a friend once, but he had moved away. She just didn't make friends easily.

"Hi, Emma!" one of the girls called.

They had seen her! Were they going to the same place? Would they see the cookie box lying there, shamefully empty?

"You going to the warehouse?" One of them, a girl named Saunders, was standing in front of her, holding three boxes of cookies. The other two were standing there panting after running down the hill, each holding cookies.

"Yes," said Emma, "I was—"

"Come on!" said Saunders. She looked at Emma's empty hands.

"Uh . . ." said Emma.

"Yes?" The girl turned back.

"Could I buy a box of those cookies? I forget to get—"

"Sure. Here, you don't have to buy it, take it."

Oh, no, not on your life. "I have the money. Here," said Emma rapidly. She handed it to Saunders, who looked indifferent as she handed her a box of Oreo cookies. Emma looked around. Two of them had Oreos. One, a small, frail person named Ketchum, held a box of Fig Newtons.

Something about this made Emma laugh, again silently. Ketchum looked terrified, but then Ketchum always looked terrified, never more so than when she stood to read one of her compositions, which were always considered brilliant. Whenever Ketchum was informed of this, she always looked as though the teacher had hit her in the face.

Emma stopped laughing before she gave Ketchum a heart attack, and smiled at her. Ketchum smiled back, exposing teeth so braced they looked like the Brooklyn Bridge.

"Let's go!" said Saunders, obviously the leader of this bunch.

The other girl was named Goldin. She looked totally unlike, but tried always to be exactly like, Saunders. She followed Saunders everywhere, dressed like her, smiled and laughed the same, even imitated Saunders' tic, which was unfortunate because Saunders had a tic and a half, a gruesome one which contorted her entire face for the length of its gyration and made her mouth look like a train going off its rails for a second, then back on again into an even stranger smile.

What a bunch, thought Emma, as she fell into step beside Ketchum. And yet look at me. What am I? I'm a fat black girl who hates the world, she thought relentlessly, and on the other hand, I am going to try to do something good.

They walked toward the river. At the bottom of Seventy-ninth Street, they turned. There was an alley. Down the alley they could see the warehouse. They all stopped.

"Did you see that guy on TV?" Saunders asked Emma.

"Yes. I called him."

"Saunders called him for us!" said Goldin proudly.

"I thought we ought to look into this," said Saunders importantly.

Ketchum said nothing, but looked more terrified than ever. Emma noted the "we" and felt she had invaded a gang. Now that she thought about it, she had seen these three together around school. She looked at Ketchum in wonder. What could this mouse get out of hanging around with the other two?

Saunders seemed nervous. She was looking at the warehouse, and Goldin was looking at her, waiting.

"Let's get on with it," said Emma, and plowed ahead.

She felt the startled motion from Saunders as she followed, something she was not used to doing. Goldin ran ahead a little, as though to make up for Saunders' sudden inadequacy as a leader. Ketchum looked as if she wanted to run the other way, but she came, slowly, hugging her Fig Newtons like a life raft.

Emma got to the door. There, indeed, was the smallest sign in the world, and it said HERE. She pushed open the metal door. There was an empty room with another metal door. She could see a small sign on that one. She poked her head in. The room was totally empty, with high windows through which slanted a sooty sunlight.

She walked across to the other door. The sign said: INSIDE THIS DOOR. PLEASE CLOSE FIRST DOOR. Goldin read over her shoulder and ran back to close the first door. Emma waited, and when they were all standing in front of the door, she opened it.

An enormous welling up of noise greeted her. The door opened onto the biggest room she had ever seen, and it was filled with kids. They were everywhere. Some were up on high benches that looked like bleachers at a parade. Most were standing or milling around. It looked like a political convention.

Emma looked at her companions. Saunders and Goldin stood there with their mouths hanging open. Ketchum looked as though she wanted to turn into a bat and fly away.

"Close the door and register over here," said a voice out of the delirium.

Emma saw a girl sitting at a card table. In front of her was an open ledger.

Goldin closed the door. They went over to the table. The noise in the room was unbelievable.

"Put your cookies in there and sign your names here,"

said the girl. She smiled. She spoke as though she had done this millions of times.

"New members?" she asked.

The four of them nodded dumbly.

"If you know your brigade name, put it down next to your name. If you don't know it, tell me where you live and I'll tell you which one you're in."

Emma signed her name and wrote Anne Frank Brigade after it. The others were being told one after the other that they too were in the Anne Frank Brigade.

Emma gestured with the cookies.

"Put them in these baskets," the girl said, and gestured toward a row of huge baskets, each with the name of a school on it.

"What does that mean?" asked Emma.

"We deliver these to the lunchrooms of various schools. The kids will get them for lunch tomorrow."

Emma nodded. So far so good. Nothing wrong with feeding people.

"Now what?" she asked. I hope to God they don't give you a physical, she thought. She had visions of all the Gauloise-smoking, sickly-looking men in the French Underground. God knows, *they* didn't have to be healthy. "Are there any requirements for joining this?" she asked. Better know them now.

"Children come first," said the girl simply. "The only requirement is that you believe this with all your heart. This is the essence of the movement."

"What does that mean?" asked Saunders. She pushed herself forward a bit, as though she felt Emma was taking over.

"We believe that if every decision made on this earth were first put to the test of one question, 'Is this good for children?' and the decision makers were forced to make decisions that would be good for children, there would only be good decisions made."

"Oh," said Saunders.

"I'll have to think about that," said Emma. I never thought of that, she said to herself. It'll take weeks for me to think that out, with all its ramifications. She felt profoundly irritated that these people had thought of something she hadn't. Not that it seemed like a bad idea —still, one had to be sure, and one could only be sure by thinking everything out carefully.

"Yes," said Saunders hurriedly, "we'll have to examine that." She wasn't letting Emma get ahead of her.

Goldin nodded, cowlike, and Ketchum suddenly, for some strange reason, looked radiant.

"See those signs?" asked the girl.

They all nodded. Signs were bobbing around just like the ones at conventions.

"One of them says Anne Frank Brigade. Go find that one and then stay with those people."

Emma began to wade her way through the crowd. There were plenty of blacks, that's for sure. A dark boy suddenly gave her the power salute.

She raised her arm and gave it back, but tentatively, because she hadn't been ready. She turned just in time to see Saunders nervously doing the same thing, Goldin too, and Ketchum, looking bug-eyed. Emma began to laugh to herself. Scared, old honky scared. She looked around the whole room. There were a lot of blacks and it made her feel good. The majority seemed to be white, but there were enough black faces to make her feel they wouldn't be ignored.

There seemed to be only six people standing under the sign saying Anne Frank Brigade.

"Hello," said Emma.

"Hello." A bespectacled boy held the sign. He looked at her with dull eyes.

"We were told to come here and stand," said Emma.

"Do you live in this section?" asked an eager-looking girl. She had long brown hair and looked friendly.

"Yes," said Saunders. She pushed herself ahead as though she'd had about enough of Emma's leadership. "We all heard Harrison Carter on television and we've joined up." She looked proud and stalwart.

"Terrific! My name's Cathy. This is Jim." She pointed to the sign holder, who smiled. "This is Alice, Nancy, Lisa, and Pippy. We're glad you're here. We're the smallest group in the whole thing. I don't know why. It seems like there are thousands of kids on East End. I don't know what's the matter with them. Maybe they didn't see the show, or maybe nobody has contacted them."

"Has anyone gone around the apartment houses?" asked Saunders. Goldin's eyes gleamed with gladness that her leader had finally come up with something intelligent.

"We have to be careful. You see, if it gets out that there is such a thing as the Children's Army, adults wouldn't go for the whole idea. In fact, we think they'd hate it. They would put a stop to it immediately. So we can't just approach everyone, somebody might be a squealer."

Emma nodded. Imagine anyone approaching Willie. He'd dance right in and tell his mother, who would tell his father, who would call the police.

"Order," said a voice. Emma looked up and saw that a pile of crates had been made into a podium. Harrison Carter was sitting on the top crate banging two pieces of wood together. I wonder where you buy gavels, thought Emma. It would be terrific to get a gavel.

"We don't have much time, as you know, because we cannot all disappear for a long time without people noticing. The first thing today is a minute of silence in memory of two innocent victims, Clifford Glover and Claude Reese, shot down in the streets by policemen when they were only ten and fourteen."

They all bowed their heads. There was silence in that

there was no talking—a little rustling, but no talking. During the minute, Emma kept her eyes closed. She bit her lip in mounting excitement. They're really doing it! Maybe we can really do something! He's hitting right where he should, right at the stupidity of adults, right at the fact that children have no rights at all, and not only that, can lose their lives because of stupid adults!

"We will never forget," said Harrison Carter. They all looked up.

"Today," said Harrison, "we are sending out three committees to talk to parents. One will discuss Helen Mason, six times admitted to six different hospitals for fractures of the arms, broken legs, bruises of the abdomen, and a smashed hand. Helen Mason is a battered child. Her parents have been getting away with this. She is six years old. A committee will approach the parents this week to inform them that the police will be notified if Helen has one more bruise. There will be ten in this committee. It will be larger than most committees because of the known violence of the father. If the parents do not respond in a satisfactory way, the committee will go to the police immediately. They will contact Martin Feininger, the father of one of our members, and a fine lawyer, who has prosecuted many parents of battered children. This violence will be stopped.

"The next committee will go to the home of Charles Tyson. Charles Tyson is being driven crazy by his mother. His father is dead. His mother will not let him out of the house except to go to school and come back. He has no freedom. He is thirteen years old and he is not even allowed to close the door to his room. The committee will inform Mrs. Tyson that an appointment has been made for her to see a psychiatrist about this situation. If she does not agree to go voluntarily, three committee members will escort her personally to the doctor's office. If she says she will call the police, the committee will say go ahead. If she does call the police, the committee will say they are friends of Charles Tyson's and they will never, under any circumstances, divulge the fact of the existence of the Children's Army. At all times, whenever confronted, each member of this Army must and will say that he or she is only acting out of personal feeling and friendship for the child involved.

"The third committee will go to the house of Lois Babson. Lois is the two-year-old sister of one of our army. The parents of this two-year-old have bought a device which rings a terrible clanging bell every time the child wets the bed. Her sister feels and this committee concurs that this is no way to toilet-train somebody, that with sympathy and patience Lois will learn to be toilet-trained, and that this barbaric arrangement should stop immediately. The committee will approach Mr. and Mrs. Babson, tell them that they are confiscating the instrument, and why. They will inform the Babsons that they will take said instrument back to the store, get a refund, and return the money to the Babsons.

"Next Friday we will send out three new committees. Each brigade must get complaints from its members and submit them. All complaints are processed as fast as possible. Anyone registering a complaint should understand that the committee acting on the complaint will use all restraint, so that the parents of the complainer do not turn against him or her. The committee members are never rude, never violent, always logical, always speak quietly, and always have a back-up adult who can be brought in at the last moment to embarrass the parents into listening. It will always appear that the committee is just a group of personal friends acting on the behalf of the complainer. We will have Report now on the three committees that went out last week." He paused dramatically. "J. Colson reporting on Committee 1."

J. Colson was a large, blond girl. Her hair kept getting in her eyes as she read the short report.

"Committee 1 went to the home of Jack Kelly, whose complaint was brought to us by his younger brother, Tom Kelly, a member. Complaint was as follows: that Jack Kelly, blind since an accident in the home when he was eight, now sixteen years old, was being kept home as a servant by his father, a drunkard. Jack Kelly is made to cook all the meals, do all the cleaning, and is not allowed to go to school. Jack Kelly wants to go to school. The committee was large because of the drunkenness of the father. They took with them an official of the Lighthouse for the blind, the mother of one of our members. Report of the committee is that Jack Kelly is now in a school for the blind, learning Braille, and he plans to attend college.

"Mr. Kelly has been reported to the police four times for drunkenness. He does not know who is reporting him, but he has had to change his habits somewhat. He will never be a good father, in the opinion of this committee, but he is nervous now to think that his sons have friends who can bring people into the house to embarrass him. He was mortified by the adult who went with us. He said he had always wanted Jack to go to school, an out-and-out lie, and that he certainly would comply. As we all know, none of this is important. What is important is that Jack Kelly is no longer a slave."

A great roar of applause went up. "Reporting on Committee 2 is Harvey Allen," said Harrison Carter when the applause had been silenced by his clacking the two pieces of wood together.

Harvey Allen was a fat, boneless sort of fellow wearing a Norwegian sweater.

"Committee 2 went to the home of Mary Ann Boniface, one of our members. Mary Ann has been subjected to the advances of an exchange student from Italy who is living in the home for a year, while Mary Ann's brother lives in Italy. Mary Ann is fifteen. She has told her parents that the boy has tried to rape her four times and that when she comes home from school she has to fight him off. The father, who likes to have the boy around, will not listen, and the mother, who likes the boy to help with the chores, will not listen. The committee informed the Bonifaces that they would contact the Institute of Foreign Exchange, which arranged for the boy's visa, unless the Bonifaces agreed voluntarily to send the boy back to Italy. Mr. Boniface said that his daughter was lying. It was the opinion of this committee, having known and worked with Mary Ann Boniface, that she was not a liar. We told the Bonifaces the facts, brought the Italian student into it, and talked to him until he finally admitted that he thought all American girls were that way, from American movies, and that he thought she would think he wasn't a man if he didn't do this. He finally came to understand that this kind of behavior not only was not required of him but was definitely not wanted by Mary Ann and was, in fact, making her hate him. Mary Ann then agreed that if he changed and stopped all that nonsense, he could stay on. The Bonifaces were told that they should know that among her friends Mary Ann has never been known to lie."

Another roar of applause went up. Emma was stunned by it all. These people acted as if they had been doing this for a hundred years, and doing it well.

"How long has this Army been in existence?" she whispered to Cathy.

"Five years. It started when Harrison Carter was eleven. He's sixteen now."

"Reporting for Committee 3 is Sissy Hendriks."

Sissy Hendriks was small and ratty-looking, with a speech impediment.

"Committee 3 had bad luck. We went to the home of Jimmy Madden, one of our members, whose father is a down-and-out punch-drunk prize fighter by the name of Mad Dog Madden. Mr. Madden was not in the least interested in what we had to say and simply tried to beat up all twelve of us. He has beaten up Jimmy for years, so that Jimmy stutters badly and his left arm doesn't work very well, because years ago Mr. Madden broke it. It was never set properly, and healed crooked.

"Jimmy is fifteen. Next year he can get a job and move away. He wants to continue with his schooling, but living with Mad Dog and being afraid is making him unable to concentrate on his schoolwork. Arrangements have been made to have Jimmy live in the home of another of our members, Jake Matthews. Mrs. Matthews runs a dry-goods store, she likes kids, and she can use Jimmy's help in the store after school. The twelve committee members were treated for bruises and cuts at Saint Vincent's Hospital, after Mr. Madden tried to throw all of us down the steps. Mr. Madden's only response to Jimmy's moving out was: 'Good riddance.' I say good riddance to Mr. Madden and to all parents like him!"

Sissy Hendriks raised her hand in the power salute and brought down the house. The noise was deafening. Harrison Carter had to beat his sticks together for several minutes to get everyone quiet.

"Time is up. Each brigade will gather complaints and bring them up here. Until next week then. Welcome to our new members. Children First!" Harrison also gave the salute, and there was more applause as he jumped down.

"I'm handing in the ones we have. Do any of you new members have any complaints?"

Ketchum looked as if she'd swallowed a toad. "I'll have to think about this," said Saunders, borrowing Emma's line and looking vastly important. Goldin nodded as though Saunders spoke for her too.

"I . . ." Emma began.

"Yes?" asked Cathy.

"Is any kind of complaint valid?" asked Emma.

"Yes. I mean, if you want the wallpaper in your room changed, or something, the committee takes a dim view of that. In general, the children who qualify are being hurt, either now or in the future, by something the parents are doing."

Emma looked uncertain.

"Want to think about it?" asked Cathy.

Emma nodded gratefully.

"Some of our members never hand in complaints. You know, you don't *have* to. It's just that most people want to see justice done some place. I mean, that's usually what's brought them here, but I've never handed in a complaint, for instance—that's what I mean, you don't *have* to." Cathy smiled again.

"I'll take these two complaints up," she said, and went toward the pile of crates.

"Well," said Saunders to the bespectacled boy, who always looked sad. "What happens now?"

"We go home," he said quietly.

He looks miserable, thought Emma. I wonder if he handed in a complaint. His parents were ruining his personality, if nothing else.

Cathy came back. "There're a couple of things I have to tell you new members. One: never, ever tell anyone about the Children's Army. Two: if someone calls you on the phone and says the one word 'Emergency,' hang up and come to this warehouse immediately, no questions asked. And it doesn't matter if you're in the middle of a family dinner either. Three: never discuss the Army over the telephone or any place you could be overheard. Parents listen all the time. Four: report injustice to a child whenever you see it, but do not act independently. We've found that we have strength in numbers. No one member is strong enough by himself or herself to accomplish anything. You will only get surrounded and beaten down by adults, and then you'll find yourself confessing. None of us want that, because that could blow the whole thing sky-high."

"Does the Children's Army use violence at any time,

in any way?" Emma decided to find out a few things *she* wanted to know, instead of being told things like a dummy.

"Never. Not in any way. Numbers are what we rely on, and the embarrassment of parents when caught by children. It almost always works. When it doesn't, we rely on getting sympathetic adults into the picture, which will always embarrass the parents. These adults never know of the existence of the Army. They think each case is an individual thing and that the committee members involved are friends, personal friends of the victim. That way they never find out about us."

"Are there any dues?" Ketchum managed to say something. She looked as though she immediately regretted it.

"Yes. One quarter a week from each person. That's a dollar a month. People who don't have it don't pay it. People who have more give more. The money is taken in a steel box to a savings bank midtown. The account is listed in the name of the Child of the Month Club. The three officers elected each year can deposit and withdraw; no one else."

"Suppose one of them is a crook?" asked Emma.

"I doubt that he would be unanimously elected, which is what has to happen for someone to become an officer. There cannot be one dissenting vote. We vote for weeks each year." Cathy smiled again. She smiled a lot. "So far, it hasn't happened.

"I'll see you guys next week if you come back. If you don't come back, by the way, you still mustn't talk. The Army doesn't use violence, but it does use what we call harassments." She laughed.

"What are they?" asked Emma.

"You'll find out quick enough if you talk."

"What happens?"

"I don't think you ever want to find out."

"What?" Emma couldn't stand it. "If you're violent to each other, it's still violence!"

"No. No violence. How would you like it, for instance, if you were turning in an A paper and a D paper was substituted?"

"Oh," said Emma. "Things like that?"

"Things like that," said Cathy. "Or have all your clothes taken out of your closet. Try and explain that to your parents!"

"That's stealing," said Emma, feeling complacent. They could be caught if they did that.

"Suppose the clothes were brought back mysteriously and put back in the closet. That would be even harder to explain."

Emma was silenced. So were Saunders, Goldin, and Ketchum. They all stood there, not knowing what to do.

"Brigade meeting is on Wednesday every week," said Cathy. "It's in the park, weather permitting, or we go to my house."

They all nodded.

"Why don't you guys go pay your dues if you want to?" Cathy smiled so brightly that it seemed only the natural thing to go over to the card table and hand a dollar bill to the girl there, who put it into a strongbox. Ketchum whispered frantically to Goldin, who produced another dollar and gave it to Ketchum, who gave it to the girl.

Everyone was going. A boy with a lapel pin that said MONITOR on it stopped them at the door.

"Wait," he said.

"Why?" asked Saunders.

"We can't be seen leaving in droves. People will wonder what goes on here. Let the eight that just left get ahead a bit." He ducked his head out the door and back in again. "Okay, you can go now."

Once out on the street, they walked silently, four abreast, each sunk in her thoughts.

Emma felt as if her hair were standing on end, being pushed out by the surprise in her brain. These people were really doing something! She looked sideways at the others. Ketchum was watching her feet. Goldin was chewing a fingernail. Saunders was pursing her lips and frowning like Judge Learned Hand. The tic took over suddenly. Emma watched the evolution of it in amazement. Extraordinary.

"I think," said Saunders.

"Yes?" said Goldin.

"They seem like a good outfit." Having delivered herself of this pompousness, she stared straight ahead.

"We," whispered Ketchum.

"What?" asked Saunders.

"We joined. We're a good outfit, not they."

Saunders looked at her. "True," she said.

It came in on Emma then that she actually had joined. She became possessed immediately of a desire to get out. Here she was, a person who had never belonged to any group, not even a group of friends, joining up with a bunch of crackpots. Suppose her father ever found out about this? That's what he'd call them, a bunch of crackpots. That's what he called everybody. She had an image of her father being confronted by a committee. He'd have the police at the house in ten minutes. He'd have the whole Army up in front of the Grand Jury in twenty minutes. One word out of their mouths: "Mr. Sheridan, we understand that you are not sympathetic to your daughter becoming a lawyer, or, for that matter, to your son becoming a dancer—" That's as far as they would get, and that committee would committee no more, they would have just committeed themselves to death.

"Do you think?" began Saunders.

"Yes?" asked Goldin.

"Do you think the four of us could get together and talk about this thing?"

"I think *somebody* better talk about it," said Emma.

"You don't mean it?" Saunders stopped in her tracks,

as did they all, and looked at Emma.

"Oh, no, I didn't mean . . ." Emma suddenly realized they thought she was going to spill the beans. "I didn't mean that. I'm not going to tell."

They walked on. "I mean, I want to talk." Here she was, Emma, reduced to having to say she wanted not only to be part of this big group, this Army, but also to be part of this small group. Me, she thought, me, the non-joiner?

"What about Monday?" asked Saunders. "We'll meet after school and go to the park."

"Great!" said Goldin, who would have given her life to meet Saunders every day after school.

"Okay?" Saunders looked at Ketchum and Emma. They nodded. "See you then," said Saunders, and turned at her corner. Goldin went after her, and Emma and Ketchum watched them walking away hurriedly, their heads together as they went up the block.

"I live on the corner," said Emma.

"I live over on York," said Ketchum.

They walked along saying nothing, until they got to the corner.

"I'll see you," said Emma.

"Okay," said Ketchum, and ducking her head, she ran.

Emma felt as though she'd been through World War II, and it was now only five by the clock in the lobby.

She and Willie almost collided at the elevator. "Ho,

Emma!" said Willie loudly, dancing around.

"Stop making a fool of yourself in the lobby," said Emma.

Willie kept right on dancing. He seemed to be doing something different, as though he were trying out something new and couldn't get it right. He paid no attention to Emma.

"Can't you see people looking at you?" Emma whispered hoarsely in his ear.

Willie turned around and looked at the woman waiting for the elevator. She smiled at him. Just for that, he did a break for her.

"Oh, for God's sake," said Emma. The elevator doors opened and they got in. The woman was evidently waiting to go to the basement, so she didn't.

Willie kept dancing in the elevator.

"I know something you don't know that's going to change your whole life," said Emma, grinning evilly at him.

"I know something you don't know that's going to change my life too," said Willie happily. Wait till I pass that audition and get that job, and then what old Emma going to say.

"What?" asked Emma.

"I ain't telling," said Willie.

"Have you done something?" asked Emma darkly, not knowing exactly what she meant herself.

"I ain't done nothing," said Willie, trying to dance up the wall again. How did that Donald O'Connor do it?

"You're going to wreck this elevator!" yelled Emma.

The door opened. Emma walked out. Willie danced past her. He stuck his key in the door and opened it. "I'm home!" he yelled cheerfully.

"Oh, for God's sake," said Emma, trudging in behind him.

At the dinner table, a battle was raging over Emma's head. Her mind was up on a barricade she had helped the Children's Army put up across East End Avenue. She was, naturally, leading her troops, with Saunders as First Lieutenant and Ketchum as Water Boy. She set the scene carefully. It was the early-morning rush-for-taxi time.

"Okay, guys! Here they come!" Emma had on a large plumed helmet. The plan was to scoop up all the fathers as they left for work, starting with the Mayor. At the other end of East End she fantasied another barricade topped by Harrison Carter in the uniform of a Zouave. They would catch the Mayor as he left Gracie Mansion. It was all timed to the second.

"Your father wants to know where you were this afternoon, Willie."

"Fooling around," whispered Willie.

Where had he been? Emma let her mind sway into reality for a minute, but only for a minute; life in fantasy was too compelling. The Mayor's long black car had just turned slowly out of the driveway of Gracie Mansion. It turned downtown instead of up, meaning that she, General Emancipation Sheridan of the First Children's Army, was going to do the capturing! "Get ready," she said to Saunders, whose jaw muscles tensed. Goldin peered over Saunders' shoulders. Ketchum's hat fell over her eyes and she dropped the water bucket.

"Willie. You weren't just fooling around for two hours." Mrs. Sheridan's voice was soft. She seemed to be pleading with Willie to tell the truth.

"Come on now, son. Were you playing ball?" Mr. Sheridan sounded hopeful.

The long black car came slowly down East End, headed for the entrance to the East River Drive. General Sheridan raised her head to examine the sandbags piled ten high and four deep across the avenue. Not a chink! They'd get him this time. Her mind skipped ahead to getting the Mayor out of his car, leading him down to the warehouse, proudly, into the room full of screaming, admiring, stunned kids. Surely they would make her the head of the Army.

"I was over to Dipsey's," mumbled Willie.

"Dipsey's? His apartment?" Mrs. Sheridan sounded horrified.

"You mean you went all the way over to Fifty-eighth

Street? By yourself?" Mr. Sheridan sounded torn between pride and anger.

Emma came to enough to watch Willie nod. What were they going to do to him, the little bugger, traipsing all over town by himself, only seven years old?

"Willie! You can't do that!" Mrs. Sheridan looked genuinely frightened. "How did you get there?"

"I took the bus." Willie didn't seem to know what was going on. He seemed confused.

"You mean your brother didn't even call you and tell you the child was there?" Mr. Sheridan glared at Mrs. Sheridan. "That irresponsible—"

"You can't blame Dipsey if Willie just showed up," said Mrs. Sheridan. "What were you doing there?" She looked at Willie.

"I had a lesson." Willie took his life in his hands to say, "He's getting me ready for an audition."

"That does it," said Mr. Sheridan. "This stupidity has gone far enough. What's your damned brother's phone number?"

"William!"

"Daddy, he didn't do nothing bad!" Willie was on the verge of tears. "Dipsey just helping me, that's all!"

Mr. Sheridan slammed his napkin down and got up from the table. "That will be just about enough help from him. Is it in your phone book? I'm calling him right now and put a stop to this!"

"Daddy, please." Willie scrambled off his chair and

after his father down the hall. Mr. Sheridan walked with heavy purpose back to his den.

"William!" Mrs. Sheridan looked helplessly at Emma.

"He got home safe anyway," said Emma, suddenly feeling a kinship with her brother which she had never felt before and which surprised her.

"He could have been killed, or run over, or gotten lost, or—" Mrs. Sheridan couldn't seem to decide whether she should sit there talking to Emma or get up and run down the hall. A noise could be heard coming from the den.

Martha came in. "What's Willie screaming about?" she asked, a frown settling uncertainly on her freckled face.

Mrs. Sheridan got up and went down the hall.

"You the only one for dessert, or they coming back?" Martha put down an apple pie in front of Mrs. Sheridan's place.

Emma didn't bother to answer, because at that moment the long black car in her mind found a way out by turning west onto Eighty-first Street. The Mayor had bypassed the barricade completely! General Emancipation Sheridan had just been made a fool of in front of everybody!

She cut herself a piece of pie, slipped it on one of the plates stacked at her mother's place, put it in front of her own place, and started to eat.

Into her mind came: *We must report injustice when-*

ever we see it. It must be a question of a child being hurt now or being hurt sometime in the future.

Emma put down her fork. Wasn't Willie being hurt? Was his future being hurt? He felt so, but was it true?

She got up and walked down the hall to the den. Her father was talking on the phone as she came into the room. Willie was crying his eyes out in his mother's arms.

"And furthermore I don't want to see your face around here any more. Never mind giving dancing lessons. Go give dancing lessons to some kid whose father doesn't care what happens to him. Leave my kid alone. He's had enough of your damned lessons. He's going to grow up a normal kid, and without any help from you!" Mr. Sheridan slammed down the phone.

Willie wailed as though his legs had been cut off. Mrs. Sheridan hugged him, trying to comfort him.

"This is unfair," said Emma.

Mrs. Sheridan looked up, surprised. Mr. Sheridan, who had been in the process of pacing the floor, stopped.

"You can't do this to him," said Emma.

Willie stopped crying in utter amazement.

"Great," said Mr. Sheridan. "Just great. Now we hear from the peanut gallery. Unfair, is it? I'll tell you what's fair, and what's fair is that I raise my son my own way without interference from you or anybody else!"

"You're not doing the right thing," said Emma. She was beginning to think she had made a mistake. She'd opened her mouth before she realized she was going to be in a knock-down, drag-out fight with her father.

"Don't talk to me about the right thing!" Her father's voice sounded like the bellow of an elephant. "I'll tell you what is the right thing and what is the wrong thing. Who do you think you are, talking to your father like that! I'm your father and don't you forget it! I decide what is right in this house and I don't need any back talk from squirts. Get out of here. I don't want to look at your face!"

Emma went back to the dining room. She had forgotten a cardinal rule of the Children's Army. *Never try to solve a problem by yourself. There is power in numbers.*

She finished her piece of pie and had another. She could hear the low mumble of voices from the den.

She considered briefly, very briefly, walking back into the den and presenting herself to her father as an *amicus curiae;* that is, a friend of the court, meaning someone who volunteers information on a point of law in a case in which he is not directly involved.

In fantasy, she watched her father throw a chair at her head for her trouble.

Steadily, she finished the whole pie. She walked back to her room. The door to the den was closed and all she heard was a mumble of voices and an occasional wail from Willie.

Her room felt wonderful to her, as usual. She looked around with satisfaction. Certainly there were books piled every which way, but what did it matter? It gave the place a warm, understanding look. She couldn't fathom why Martha always gave a shriek of horror whenever she came in to clean. It wasn't as though there was a lot of dirt around, like old candy wrappers or something like that. There were just books and more books, filling the bookshelves, piled on the floor, under the bed, crawling along the windowsill, and falling off the chair.

The room had soft blue walls, one of which Emma had covered with an Indian bedspread. Everything else seemed colorless, being different shades of beige. There was a bed, a desk, a chair, her old armchair, a small television, and a radio with an alarm which woke her every morning with news, generally featuring the murders of the night, to which she listened as she dressed. She imagined to herself that she would always live this way, even after she had grown up and moved away from her family. She planned to have exactly the same room wherever she was, because this room was *her*. No matter what happened out there in the rest of the world, she felt totally comfortable once she got into this room and closed the door. She wondered if Golda Meir had a room like this, or Simone de Beauvoir.

She turned on the television and sat down in her armchair. She piled her schoolbooks next to the chair.

She sped through her homework. Homework was a snap to her. It had always been easy. The thing was to get through it fast, so she could concentrate on what to do about Willie. She left the television picture on with the volume turned down so she couldn't hear the sound.

For one fleeting moment she wondered at herself that she cared what happened to Willie, but it didn't seem strange, even though it was different and she knew it was a change for her.

It seemed, on the contrary, relaxing, a natural feeling, as though all the old hates and jealousies had been the strange feelings.

She wondered if this was all false. Maybe she was just using his case to create a complaint for the Children's Army.

Was it a genuine case for a committee? She put down her homework. There was no way not to think about Willie, try as she might.

She decided that she would try to be perfectly objective. She would try to think about Willie as though he were not her brother, as though he were one of the cases mentioned by Harrison Carter.

She imagined Harrison Carter up on his packing crate. "The committee visited the home of one Willie Sheridan, the brother of a member. Willie is being persecuted by his father. The only thing that Willie wants in life is to go away to summer stock this summer and do what he wants to do, and that's dance. His father thinks dancing is sissy."

Emma stopped herself. Is that what her father thought? All he had actually said was that blacks didn't have to do the kinds of things they used to have to do, like dance and sing. What was it that her father objected to so much? What was her father so mad about?

I don't have enough information, she thought sudenly. I better find out what I'm talking about before I bring this thing up. She went back to her homework.

● ●

"Come on, dear, I have to get you to bed." Mrs. Sheridan was poking Willie, who had fallen asleep after crying.

Willie opened one eye and saw his father looking at him. Memory flooded back, accompanied by horror. His father had actually screamed at Dipsey on the phone. His father had told Dipsey once and for all that he had to leave Willie alone. He had told Willie that he was not to see Dipsey, or to meet him secretly, or, in fact, to have anything to do with him, even talk to him on the phone.

Willie groaned and closed his eye again.

"Come on, dear, you're too big to pick up," Mrs. Sheridan said warmly.

His father came over and scooped him up as though he were so many throw pillows. Mrs. Sheridan opened the door to the den and his father went down the hall carrying him in his arms. He carried him into his room and put him down on the bed. Mrs. Sheridan stood in the doorway.

"I want you to know, son, that I am doing the best for you." His father stood by the bed heavily, awkwardly.

Willie looked up at him with bleary eyes. This guy has to be kidding, he thought. He can't be talking about me. The best for me is what Dipsey can give me.

"This is just a passing thing. As you get older, you'll go through many things like this. It would be unfair to you if I were to take this seriously. When you get older and you have more judgment, I'm sure that you will make wiser decisions about your life."

"I'm not going to be any different," said Willie.

"I'm sure you will see, later, that I was right," said his father, unperturbed. He smiled. "I think, probably, when you're eighteen, you'll even look back on this and thank me." With that, his father turned and left the room.

Thank him! Willie lay there, stunned. Thank him for messing up everything!

His mother said, "Get your clothes off, dear, and get into your pajamas. It's bedtime." She smiled and closed the door.

Willie lay there like a caught fish. They talk like crazy people, he thought. He wants me to thank him and she says it's bedtime, when here I am with nothing left in my life. I could jump right out the window—that's how much I care about anything. He tried to envision a life without dancing a step. He saw himself plodding to school. He saw himself plodding home from school, plodding back to school the next morning and home again the next afternoon.

No. Life like that would be one long hell. He thought of never seeing Dipsey. He thought of having no dreams. What would there be to look forward to? What was all this, anyway? His father couldn't possibly be saying that he, Willie, wasn't ever to dance again. Could he?

He thought of his father's face as he'd talked to Dipsey on the phone. That's just what his father was saying.

His father was saying that he, Willie, wasn't to dance any more, wasn't to think about it any more, wasn't to want anything to do with it, was not to dream.

Fat chance.

Mrs. Sheridan opened the door. "Come on, darling, get your PJ's on."

"Mama?"

"Yes?"

"What's the matter with Daddy?"

Mrs. Sheridan came into the room and hurriedly shut the door after herself. "Why, darling, what do you mean?" She looked nervous.

"What's got him so angry?"

"He's not angry, dear. He's concerned about you."

"Well, tell him not to be concerned about me."

"He wants the best for you. He loves you."

"He don't love me. If he loved me, then he'd want me to do what I want to do."

"That's not always so. What about children who want

to do something that's bad for them? Their fathers have to watch out for them and see that—"

"What's bad about dancing?"

"Well, nothing at the moment, but if you have a life that's like the life dancers have to live, then—"

"Mama, that's all I want. I just want to do what Dipsey does."

"Honey, Dipsey is a man. He can take care of himself."

"Mama, didn't you tell me all about Granddaddy and how he was in vaudeville and how your mama was and what it was like?"

"Yes, but that was a long time ago. That was a different world. And it wasn't always pleasant. There were times we didn't have enough to eat, or any place to stay, and no money at all."

Willie, who didn't give a hoot about eating or money, pushed on. "But nothing bad happened, did it, Mama? I mean, nobody was killed and everybody was okay?"

"It's a long, hard life, Willie. There's a lot of heartbreak in it."

Willie was sitting there with his heart broken, so this didn't make any sense to him.

"You're too young, darling. You don't know enough about life yet."

Willie was thinking hard. If only they wouldn't cut it all off completely. "Mama, couldn't I just go back to having my one dancing lesson a week? I wouldn't go to Dipsey's again. He would come here. I know he would."

"Your father was mad tonight, but I'll try to talk to him when he's not so upset. It scared him, your going all the way across town like that."

"Nothing happened to me."

"But it could have." Mrs. Sheridan stood up. "Get undressed now. I'll talk to your father."

"When?"

"Soon."

"When, Mama?"

"Soon, dear." She opened the door and went out.

Willie got up and started for his closet. On the way he began to dance. He decided he was Fred Astaire and the number involved changing into pajamas. He danced his way out of his clothes and he danced his way into his pajamas.

For once, Emma didn't knock on the wall and say she'd cut his feet off. He was so tired he didn't notice. He danced his way to bed, fell into it and into sleep.

● ●

The next morning was Saturday. Willie stayed in his room all day. His mother kept coming to the door trying to get him to go out into the park, but he wouldn't budge.

Emma went to the library. She took down four enormous books from the legal section and sat with her head buried in them until it was closing time.

● ●

On Sunday, Willie went out for the Sunday paper as usual. He came back and, without a word, handed it to his father. His mother watched him as he went slowly back into his room and closed the door.

Emma was coming down the hall and saw Willlie go into his room. "William, I'm worried about Willie," she heard her mother say. "Don't be," said her father. "He'll get over it. You'll see." Emma continued on her way to the fridge.

● ●

On Monday morning, Emma, who was consuming two fried eggs, bacon, sausage, and three pieces of toast, looked over at Willie, who sat, his plate full and untouched in front of him, chewing slowly on a corner of a piece of toast, looking out the window at the river.

They were alone in the dining room. Mr. Sheridan had left for work very early, and Mrs. Sheridan wasn't awake yet.

Emma looked carefully at her brother. She noticed for the first time that his eyes were sad eyes, that his neck was thin, and that his hands, holding the toast, were small. Seven isn't really very old, she thought to herself. Maybe he doesn't know what he's doing. On the other hand, he seems to know. She could see that he must have cried during the night. His eyes were swollen. He was chewing, but the toast didn't seem to get any smaller.

"Uh, are you going to see Dipsey any more?"

Willie looked at his sister. What he didn't need this morning was any fat lip from her. "What's it to you?" he asked, then jammed the toast back into his mouth and looked at the river again.

"I don't think it's fair." Emma said this while eating a sausage.

Willie turned his head to take in his sister's curious eyes. He remembered then that she had said something similar to their father. Could he trust her?

Emma saw that her brother's eyes were deep with sadness, great brown wells ready to spill over. He seemed to be examining her as though he'd never seen her before.

"I think something should be done about it," said Emma softly, so Martha in the kitchen couldn't hear.

Willie's eyes hardened. The moment was past. "What?" he said scornfully.

"He's got to see he's wrong."

"Who?"

"Dad." Emma couldn't say Daddy. It made her feel like a pickaninny in a bad movie running across a cotton field yelling "Daddy, Daddy."

"Ha." Willie couldn't be roused from his pit. "How you expect to do that?"

"I don't know yet, but I think there's a way," said Emma mysteriously.

Willie shrugged. "He not going to change his mind. Not him."

Martha came in. "Out, out. You're going to be late. Both of you."

Willie dragged himself off the chair, picked up his briefcase, and slouched toward the door.

Definitely, thought Emma, definitely a possibility for a committee. She determined to push something through as quickly as possible, even if she was a new member, and even if her father would throw them all out the window.

● ●

Saunders and Goldin were waiting for her outside of school after her last class.

"Can you go to the park?" asked Goldin.

"Yes," said Emma.

"We'll wait for Ketchum," said Saunders.

Ketchum appeared then, all frightened and loaded down with books.

"Let's go," said Saunders.

They marched four abreast down the hill to East End, then up the avenue to the park. Nobody said a word. They walked into the park and sat down on a bench.

"I have some literature here," said Saunders, pulling a sheaf of papers out of her bag. "That girl Cathy gave it to me over the weekend. I contacted her."

Get you, thought Emma, *contacted,* like a spy movie.

"She says we ought to look this over." It turned out to be only one piece of paper, because Saunders had gotten it mixed up with her history assignment. She passed it around.

When it was Emma's turn, she saw that it had only one line written on it. It said: INNER PROGRESS BEFORE OUTER PROGRESS.

"Is that all?" asked Emma. She had thought there would be instructions, like go to the Eighty-sixth Street station of the IRT and follow a man in a gray coat.

Saunders nodded. She waited for Ketchum to finish reading the paper. Ketchum handed it back, no expression on her face.

"What does it mean?" asked Emma.

"What does it appear to mean?" asked Saunders, who seemed to be under the impression that she had turned into her own English teacher, who was well known for saying exactly that, in exactly that way.

"Oh, come off it," said Emma.

Saunders looked affronted, and Goldin leapt into the breach. "I think what Saunders means is that it's saying just what it seems to be saying. I mean, this country is always talking about progress, like new buildings, new roads, new machines, and look at the people. Nobody grows up."

Ketchum burst out laughing, inexplicably. Everybody turned to her. She stopped laughing and went back to her strange glancing around.

It was then that they all realized that Ketchum had been swiveling her head around, darting her eyes back and forth, and generally looking frightened to death ever since they came into the park.

"What's the matter with you?" asked Emma.

Ketchum started, grabbed her books, and looked ready to run out of the park.

"Wait," said Goldin. "What's the matter?"

"I'm not supposed to be here," whispered Ketchum, her eyes flying around in her head like frightened birds.

"Where?" asked Emma.

"In the park." She hugged her books.

"You supposed to be somewhere else?" Emma felt amused. Ketchum looked so tiny huddled there, her eyes flying.

"A man was murdered here," whispered Ketchum. She leaned forward so far that she almost fell, and all her books dropped.

Emma helped her pick them up, noticing as she did that Ketchum had spidery little white hands, covered with freckles. Emma was fascinated by the ugliness of them. She thought white skin ugly anyway, but Ketchum's hands took the cake. She tried to hand the books back without touching them.

"My father told me not to set foot in this park, even in the daytime." Ketchum was breathless with her own deceit.

Emma looked around. There were nannies with baby carriages, children being pushed on swings. Everything looked the way it always did.

"I think we'll be all right," said Saunders. Goldin nodded.

"But a whole bunch of guys came across from Eighty-sixth Street and killed this guy," said Ketchum.

"At night?" asked Emma.

Ketchum nodded. "Well, then," said Saunders. "What I think we ought to talk about," she continued, dismissing murder, "is whether we have any complaints. Cathy said that the best thing to do was to talk over complaints with friends and choose the really important ones, you know, so nobody is embarrassed in front of the whole brigade by some, you know, dumb complaint, like they don't like their breakfast cereal and they want it changed."

Emma laughed her silent laugh. They all watched her shaking and making no noise, until she saw them watching her. She stopped laughing and said, "That's ridiculous. Who would do that?"

"Obviously, she didn't really mean that," said Saunders, looking superior.

Emma became aware that Saunders had mean eyes. Mean eyes and a dull mind, she thought. "Obviously," she said. "Okay, who's first with a complaint?"

Nobody said a word. Everyone looked at the river as though they'd never seen it before. Ketchum must have moved, because all her books fell again. Emma helped her again.

"Uh, Saunders"—Ketchum leaned over Emma, who was picking up books—"could I speak to you privately?"

"Certainly," said Saunders. She stood up and walked over to the railing. Ketchum followed her. They stood, leaning over the river, talking.

Emma felt like a fat frog, sitting there watching them. She looked at Goldin. Goldin was watching them too. Goldin was looking only at Saunders, as usual.

"Nice day," said Emma. Goldin was too engrossed in watching her master to answer.

Saunders put an arm around Ketchum and led her back to the bench.

"This is definitely a serious problem," she said, and sat down next to Emma, making a place for Ketchum beside her. Ketchum seemed to have picked up Goldin's disease, because she looked up into Saunders' eyes adoringly.

"Ketchum's uncle is posing a problem. This uncle is her father's brother. He's out of a job all the time and is always coming over and hanging around the house, especially the afternoons, when Ketchum is home alone after school." Saunders paused for drama, checking everyone to see if they were paying attention. "This uncle makes indecent proposals to Ketchum."

Emma couldn't believe her ears. Ketchum? Who would make any kind of proposal to Ketchum, let alone indecent. She searched Ketchum's face. Was Ketchum making this up?

"Ketchum wants him stopped," finished Saunders.

"Naturally," said Goldin.

"Let's take a vote," said Saunders. "Is this serious enough for presentation?"

"Has this happened more than once?" asked Emma.

Ketchum looked petrified, but nodded.

"Is your family—are your mother and father aware of this?"

Ketchum said, "Oh, no," and tried to get to her feet, presumably to run out of the park.

"Ketchum can't tell her family," said Saunders. "She's tried, but she can't talk to them, about that or about anything else."

"Would they be violent if approached by a committee?" Emma pressed on. As she did this, she was thinking of her own family and how she would answer these questions.

"I don't think so," said Ketchum. "They never hit me or anything."

Who would hit a frightened thing like you, thought Emma.

"Let's take a vote," said Saunders. "I vote yes, that

this is serious enough." She raised her hand.

Goldin raised hers immediately, then Emma.

Ketchum gave a sort of little screech. "Oooo, you mean they're going to come to my house?"

"That's what you want, isn't it?" asked Goldin.

"Oooo, I don't know," squealed Ketchum.

"We'll come back to that later," said Saunders. "Goldin, you have a problem, I believe?"

"Yes," said Goldin. "I have three brothers. My father thinks everything they do is wonderful. My mother is dead. Like, when they bring home report cards, he makes a big chazzerei over every B they get, and when I bring home my report card, which is all A's, he doesn't say a damn thing, like that's what I should get, that's what's expected of me. And my brothers can't stand me, like they trip me all the time and hide my clothes so I'm late for school, and they steal all my pens and pencils and notebooks, and my sweaters. One of them likes to dress in girl's clothes and he's all the time stealing my sweaters."

"And you can't talk to your father about this, can you?" asked Saunders, prompting.

"God, no. He thinks the boys hung the moon. When I was little, I couldn't even say one of them hit me, even when I was bleeding from it. He wouldn't believe me, he would make out like I walked into a door or something. They never do anything wrong as far as he's concerned."

"So there would be your father and three boys for the

committee to face?'' Saunders seemed to have thought about all this before. Emma figured they had talked about it together before this.

"That's right," said Goldin. "And they're big, too. My brothers are big guys, at least two of them are—the one who likes to dress up is smaller."

"Does your father know of this tendency?" asked Emma.

"What do you mean?" asked Goldin.

"Does your father know this boy has a tendency toward transvestitism?" Emma was proud of her vocabulary.

"What?" asked Ketchum abruptly.

"Oh, right," said Goldin. "No, he doesn't know it goes on all the time. He saw him once dressed up for a school play like that and he told him he was beautiful. I tell you, anything they do is just perfect with him. They can't do any wrong."

"What do you want the committee to tell him?" asked Emma.

"I don't know, exactly," said Goldin. "I mean, he's not going to listen, I'll tell you that right now. I guess he should be told to change his attitude, but I don't think he'd listen for one minute. I mean, he doesn't see anything wrong with his attitude."

"Let's vote," said Saunders.

"On what?" asked Emma. "We have to know what she wants accomplished first."

"I think we just have to vote on whether it's serious or not," said Saunders.

"The point is," said Emma, "it has to be clear-cut that the committee can do some good, like something she could ask that the father stop doing, not just his attitude, but something he does to her." Emma knew she was right, but her heart sank as she said what she said, because wasn't it her own father's attitude that was at fault? If he would just change his attitude about Willie —but no, he had done something too. He had said that Willie couldn't take dance lessons any more. The committee could get the dance lessons reinstated.

"He would have to change everything about himself," said Goldin. "I can't see them asking for that—like, Hi, there, Mr. Goldin, go change yourself."

"The boys do things to you, though. He could be made to see that, and he could be made to stop them, right?" Emma felt triumphant at having discovered this.

Goldin nodded uncertainly. Saunders' eyes brightened. "You could tell the committee about the one who steals your clothes. Then, when they tell your father to stop him from stealing your clothes, your father will—"

"—look like a ninny and let you have it," said Emma. "I think the best thing would be to punch the physical violence. Make a lot of them tripping you and socking you and so forth. That way, even your father will have to say there's something wrong with that, but he can just chalk it off to 'boys will be boys.' It wouldn't make him look bad, which would make him turn against you."

"Right!" said Goldin. "Hey, that's brilliant! Hey, Saunders, isn't she great?" Goldin glistened her eyes at Emma.

Emma looked away. She didn't want Goldin switching from Saunders to her and following her around the halls.

"I think that's good," said Saunders, as though Emma had said something perfectly ordinary that everybody knew and that she, Saunders, just hadn't got around to saying because it was so dull. "Okay, so the proposal is that your father stop the boys from beating up on you. I vote yes." Saunders raised her hand.

Emma raised hers, and Ketchum raised hers. "Okay," said Saunders. "Anybody else?"

Since there was no one left but Saunders and herself, Emma said, "How about you?"

"I'm thinking about something," said Saunders. "I don't know if I'm ready yet to bring it up."

Clever, thought Emma, get them all to expose themselves before you tell anything about yourself.

"We can wait," said Emma.

"Do *you* have a complaint?" asked Saunders.

Pinned, thought Emma, right to the ass of the donkey. Okay, she said to herself, here goes nothing. She opened her mouth, but she couldn't bring herself to say anything. Three white faces leaned toward her. She had never been more aware than at this moment that they were white. She remembered one of the fears of her childhood, her fear of white faces. Her mother would laugh about it now and tell about Emma rearing back when a white face leaned down into the bassinet. Now white faces only looked weak to her, as though white people didn't have as much substance, but were so much protoplasm without much reality.

"Uh," she said intelligently. "This may be a matter for the courts." Rats. Why had she said that? She was going to look like an utter fool now, when she told the truth. "I mean, this kind of behavior should be a matter for the courts, whereas it is not, in this day and age, in the legal system we have." She was dribbling on wildly. Why couldn't she just start?

"What's the problem?" asked Goldin with a kindly look on her face.

They probably expect me to say that I live in Harlem and the rats are running all over our apartment and we have no clean drinking water.

"I live on East End at Seventy-ninth," she said, although no one had asked her, nor had anyone else given her address. "Uh, my little brother wants to be a dancer, my father doesn't want him to be." How to explain that dancing used to be something everybody tried to do because there wasn't anything else, and now, since her father was a lawyer, he wanted his son not to go down socially but to be a lawyer too and carry everybody forward. She looked at the white faces. They wouldn't have the faintest idea what she was talking about. "My father thinks it's sissy," she said finally. "My brother doesn't like to do anything in the world but dance, and my father is stopping him."

"How old is your brother?" asked Saunders.

"Seven."

"Does he dance well?" asked Goldin.

"Terrific. He's really good. See, we have an uncle who's a dancer, a professional, and he's in all the shows—"

"What's his name?" asked Goldin.

"Dipsey Bates."

"Wow! Dipsey Bates is your uncle? No kidding!" Goldin was really impressed. Even Saunders murmured something, and Ketchum's eyes got wide.

"You heard of him?"

"Sure! Everybody has. You mean, here you have an uncle in show business and your father won't let your brother—won't let him what?—dance around the house?"

"No, see, Dipsey's been giving him lessons, and Willie, that's my brother, he wants to go away to summer stock with Dipsey this summer, and my father won't let him, and now my father has even stopped the dancing lessons."

"Is he a sissy?" asked Goldin.

"Willie?" Emma thought a minute. When she thought about it in any concrete way, she realized she didn't know what a sissy was. "How do you mean?" she asked guardedly.

"Well, you know," said Goldin, "like my brother who wants to wear dresses, he's a sissy. He's afraid of everything and screams like a girl when he sees a mouse. My brothers tease him all the time and he cries."

Willie cried, but then he had a reason. Was he afraid of everything? Actually, Willie didn't seem to be afraid of anything. She, Emma, had tried to *make* him afraid on many occasions. She thought of this now with the beginnings of shame. She remembered once holding him against the sill of an open window and telling him she was going to push him out. That was only last year. All he'd done was kick her in the stomach and run down the hall. Just the other day, he had gone all the way across town by himself. Somebody afraid wouldn't do that.

"No. He's not a sissy. He just wants to do what he wants to do. He wants to dance."

"Then I think your father ought to be stopped." Goldin spoke very definitely.

"Suppose"—everybody looked at Ketchum when she spoke—"suppose he were a sissy. What difference would it make?"

Emma felt even guiltier, for having called Willie a faggot.

"I guess," said Saunders, "his father might want him to stop being one."

"Ha! My brother couldn't stop being like himself if the roof fell in on him!" Goldin laughed. "I think he's that way forever."

"I think"—they all looked at Ketchum again—"I think that whatever a person is, that's what he is, and a person wants to be the way he is." They all kept looking at her even though she'd stopped. "I don't see anything wrong with sissies anyway," she said, to get them to stop looking at her.

"Yeah," said Saunders. "Why does everybody go around all the time trying to change everybody else?" Saunders crossed and uncrossed her legs, as though philosophy made her nervous. "I have a similar problem," she said unexpectedly. "I plan to go into physics when I'm older. I'm very good at science and—"

"Yes, she is," said Goldin. "She's fantastic. You should see her in the lab!"

Saunders waited for this praise and seemed to ignore it at the same time. "—and I know exactly how I want to live my life. Believe me, it doesn't include raising a bunch of brats and washing some guy's socks. My mother keeps telling me how wonderful babies are, and it really makes me barf. I ask you, what's wonderful about a dirty diaper? You know, these guys have it good, having a wife. I wouldn't mind having a wife myself."

"That's right," said Goldin, nodding away and looking glisteny-eyed, as though she couldn't wait for Saunders to pop the question. She would have washed Saunders' socks *and* changed her diapers.

"My complaint," continued Saunders, "is just the way my mother and father *talk* to me. Whenever I mention science, it's as though I've said a dirty word. My mother actually talks right through me and says, 'Well, you'll meet a nice young doctor and then you'll be able to help him with his practice.' Can you imagine? Help him change the diapers on the patients, I suppose."

"That's the way my mother talks," said Emma, amazed that anyone else had had such an experience. "She said to me the other night, 'And you'll grow up and marry a lawyer and have two lovely children!' I keep trying to tell her I don't want two lovely children and I want to *be* a lawyer, not marry one!"

"Why don't you tell the committee about that?" Saunders seemed much more friendly to Emma.

"Same reason you don't, hot-shot," said Emma, and Saunders jumped back. "They don't *do* anything to me. It's just their attitude."

"But, Saunders, your mother *does* do things to you. She keeps introducing you to all those medical students and making you sit and talk to them." Goldin looked ready to kill Saunders' mother.

"Yeah. My dad's a doctor and he brings home all these medical students to dinner and they're all half asleep sitting around after dinner because none of them get enough sleep and my mother makes me go in and talk to them. What do they want with an eleven-year-old kid asking them about lab experiments? So they yawn at me and laugh at me a lot. And my mother really thinks I can catch a husband if I just sit there and be quiet. 'Let them talk,' she says to me. 'Let them tell you all about themselves. Don't ask about the experiments. They think you know too much. Let them remember you as a sweet child. Then when you're older, they'll see a lovely young lady and they'll be interested.' "

"Isn't that incredible?" Goldin asked Emma.

The idea of Saunders being married to anybody but Goldin was what was incredible, but Emma didn't say so. She put herself in Saunders' shoes and thought about her own father bringing home law students. She wished he would. She could learn a lot that way, but she wouldn't even be allowed in the room with them, much less allowed to talk.

"But you could say no to her, couldn't you?" asked Emma. "You could say you didn't want to talk to those medical students and that you wouldn't, couldn't you?"

Saunders considered this. "Yes. Yes, I could."

"Then I don't think that's valid. It's got to be something they make you do, or won't let you do. It can't just be attitude."

Saunders rummaged into her book bag again. "Cathy gave me some other things too. Here's one that might apply."

She handed around a list. "These are committees for study. If you're interested, you put your name down and you gather research on a particular thing, like here it says 'Legal Committee.' "

"Where?" Emma asked breathlessly. "Where does it say 'legal'?"

"Here."

"I'll do that." Emma felt something calm down inside herself. There was a place for her.

"Here's the Committee for the Study of Parental Attitudes," said Saunders. "Maybe we should go to them with problems about attitudes."

"No," said Emma, "they just study attitudes. They wouldn't do anything."

"I don't know about that," said Saunders.

She doesn't like to be crossed, thought Emma, about anything, even about something obvious like this.

Saunders seemed to read Emma's mind. "What about your brother?"

"My brother?" Emma knew full well what she meant.

"Yes," said Saunders with an edge to her voice. "Do you want the committee to come to your house?"

Emma's knees went to water. She wanted to squeal like Ketchum at the thought. She could feel her eyes darting around because she didn't want to look at Saunders.

"You chicken?" asked Saunders.

Oh-ho, thought Emma, I know now how she got to be

a leader. She makes other people do what she's afraid to do.

"What about them coming to *your* house?" asked Emma.

"We're asking you now," said Saunders coldly.

Goldin, evidently, did not like seeing her mentor in a cruel light. "Emma doesn't have to decide now, does she? I mean, it's a big decision."

"I don't want to decide now either," said Ketchum.

Emma cleared her throat, trying to fight down her fear, to regain some of the calm she had felt earlier. "I think these things should be given all due consideration. This is tantamount to making a decision to go to court. The law does not take kindly to those who are just litigation-happy."

She looked around, satisfied. They all looked at her as though they didn't know what she was talking about.

Perfect, she thought. Keep 'em guessing.

● ●

When Emma first walked into the park, Willie was on the phone with Dipsey.

"Now look, kid. I can't get into trouble with your parents. You heard what your father said."

"Dipsey, you got to teach me!"

"Baby, I ain't *got* to do nothing but dance, pay taxes,

and die. I know how you feel. It's rough, but if I were you, I'd go to your old man and have a long talk with him. Maybe this just isn't the time, you know? Maybe you just ought to wait a few years until you're older."

"Aw, please, Dipsey—"

"Don't go trying to break my heart now. I told you how I feel. Listen, baby, I got to be at rehearsal in ten minutes and it's way cross town at the Winter Garden. I'll be talking to you."

"That's right next door, practically!"

"Yeah? Well, I forgot. I'll be talking to you, baby. Hang in there!"

The phone clicked down. Willie stood there holding the receiver. A man in a raincoat waiting for the phone booth hit the glass with a quarter. "Come on out! You finished! Give somebody else a chance!"

Willie hung up, opened the door, and ran past the man. He kept running for a bit, because he wasn't even aware that he was running. He sat down on a stoop to think.

How could Dipsey say a crazy thing like that? Talk to your father. How could you talk to a mountain? How could you talk to a Boeing jet?

Dipsey knows that's stupid. He can't talk to my father either. How come he's saying that? He knows I can't do it. He want to get me off his back?

I can't get down now. If I get down now, I'll never get up.

He sat on the stoop, unconsciously tapping his feet to the rhythm of the song Dipsey had used as audition music.

An idea hit him. The idea grew and swelled into a beautiful thing in his mind, a thing he couldn't let go, a thing so wonderful that it filled his heart, moved his body up and off the stoop, pushed his feet along until they had him running down the street.

He jumped onto the Seventy-ninth Street crosstown bus. He rode to Fifth, his eyes seeing nothing but an image. He got on a Fifth Avenue bus and rode downtown to Fiftieth Street.

He started running. He skipped, he hopped, he danced around people, threaded his way through the crowd at the corner of Broadway, ran again until he was in front of the theater.

He tried one door. It was locked. The middle one was unlocked. He was in an empty lobby. He opened a door to the theater.

I'll do it, he said to himself as he slipped into the dark theater, I'll do it, I'll do it.

The stage was bare except for a piano. There were five or six men in the front rows down near the stage. The entire theater, except for one light on the stage, was dark.

"Okay!" yelled one of the men.

The piano player sat down and started a number. The

music filled the theater and took Willie's heart all the way up to the balcony.

"Next," yelled the man.

A woman came out of the wings and started singing. Willie sat down in the back row, hoping the light from the stage didn't make him visible.

I'll do it, he said to himself again. I'll just wait here and I'll do it.

The man down front stood up. He waved his hand. "Okay," he said. The piano stopped. "Thank you so much for coming," he said to the singer, who looked only mildly surprised. She turned and walked offstage.

"Get Dipsey," the man said to the piano player. "We got all these kids to try, three of them look okay. I want them to try it with him."

Willie's mouth flew open. Other kids? Over my dead body, he said to himself. I don't know how I'll do it, but I'll do it. I could run backstage—no, there must be lots of people there. Dipsey would see me. Dipsey would stop me.

Dipsey came walking out. He peered down at the man. "Hi, Fred. How you doing?"

"Hey, Dips, we got three kids we can't decide between. I thought you might help. Do a little with them and see if one grabs you. Okay?"

"Sure thing," said Dipsey. He took off his suit jacket and loosened his tie. He went toward the wings and dropped his jacket on a chair.

Willie felt his throat go dry as he watched Dipsey. He's going to dance with some other kid! I'll murder him.

"Let's do the ice-cream number," he said to the piano player. "If they can do that, they can do anything."

"Send out the first kid," yelled the stage manager, who had appeared from the wings, holding a clipboard and a pen.

The music started. Dipsey started. Willie almost forgot why he was there. As he watched Dipsey, his whole body began to move with him. More than anything in life, he loved the way Dipsey moved. He stayed in his seat, but his feet started to move with Dipsey's feet and he was doing all the same steps they had done that afternoon.

A small boy ran out of the wings and started dancing with Dipsey.

Willie looked at him coldly. His feet even stopped moving. He looked at every part of that boy's body. No, no, not like that. Stop trying to look nice.

"Easy," said Dipsey to the boy. "Take it easy, like this."

Like you told *me*, thought Willie, like *I* know how to do. The boy kept on stomping away and at the same time waving his arms like he was some show girl.

When the boy's back was turned, Dipsey managed to give the thumbs-down signal to the man in the audience.

"Okay," said the man, standing up. The piano stopped. "Thanks for coming by," he said to the kid. "You're doing real well. Keep up the lessons."

The kid skipped off like an idiot. He didn't know he'd just blown it.

The piano started again.

Dipsey started again.

Willie got up out of his seat and ran down the aisle. He ran up the steps and onto the stage. Dipsey was in the middle of a turn and didn't see him until Willie was already doing his steps.

Without missing a beat, Dipsey smiled at him and winked. "Easy-like," whispered Dipsey.

Willie moved like butter. He followed everything Dipsey did like a smaller one-and-the-same, like a small shadow come to life.

Dipsey was grinning all over himself. "Hold back," he whispered. "Don't let 'em have it yet!"

Willie held it in until he thought he would burst, but the smoothness of Dipsey and the smoothness of the piano and being there finally on that enormous stage made him say to himself, "Hold it. Hold it right this minute, or you'll never get another chance."

He danced better than he thought he ever could. "Now, baby, like I told you, we going to give it to 'em!" Dipsey's voice went from a whisper into a shout as he yelled, "Let's go, Willie, now!"

Willie danced faster than he'd ever danced, faster

even than that day in the apartment. He didn't make any mistakes and he let them have it, all right.

"Now, back down easy, baby," whispered Dipsey. "Easy, and over—and out!"

The piano stopped.

All six guys in the audience stood up and applauded. Dipsey grabbed him by the neck. "Hey, you bugger, what you doing here?"

Willie was laughing and gasping for breath and couldn't say anything, just allowed his head to be buried against Dipsey's stomach.

"Hey, fellas, you like him?" Dipsey led him over to the edge of the stage.

"If you want him, Dips, you got him. He's great!" Willie could just see a blurred shape talking.

"You hear that, Willie?" Dipsey picked him right up off the ground and threw him up in the air. "You got the job, baby!" He grabbed Willie and hugged him until Willie thought his bones would break. "You got the job!"

Willie was giggling and laughing and crying and felt like throwing up.

Dipsey led him to the edge of the stage again. "Hey, guys, this is my nephew!"

"No kidding!"

"How 'bout that?"

"Yeah," said Dipsey, grabbing Willie again and smiling the biggest grin. "Him and me are going places!"

"What's his name?" asked the man in the audience.

"Willie, this here's my Willie, my dancing Willie." Dipsey grabbed him again.

"He have an agent?"

"Yeah, me," said Dipsey, laughing. "Naw, tell you what. I'll take him to my agent."

"Okay, tell him to call us. It'll be scale anyway, and he'll have to get an Equity card."

"Don't worry. I'll get him all set up. Only small problem might be rehearsals during school hours, or costume fittings, because he's got to keep on with school."

"No problem. School's almost out for the year. Take him back there and get him measured. What's his last name?"

"Sheridan," said Willie. "Willie Sheridan."

"You tell 'em, fat lady," said Dipsey, and led him off-stage.

Willie got measured. Dipsey went onstage for rehearsal. He came back after Willie was finished.

"Listen, Willie, I don't think you're going to have any problem with your father, once you tell him you got a job and all like that, but if you want me to go with you—"

"I'm not going to tell him," said Willie.

"How can you do that? You got to tell him. Your name will be in the papers for one thing, and before that, you're going to have to be here in the afternoons to rehearse. You can't get by with that, Willie, he'll find out, and then it'll be worse!"

"I'm not going to tell him. I'm going to tell my mother."

"Oh." Dipsey smiled. "Yeah. I see what you mean. I don't blame you. Tell her—" Dipsey looked serious. "Tell her I'm going to take care of you and all. If she's got any questions, just call me. Okay?"

Willie nodded. Everything seemed simple when Dipsey said it.

"Can you get home by yourself? No, wait, I can't let you do that again. Here, wait right here a minute."

Dipsey walked onstage and over to where a group of people were standing. He was telling them something. He came back then to Willie. "Come on. You're going to like this." He took Willie by the hand and led him out the stage door.

"The director has a car and chauffeur here. He's going to let the car run you home." He led Willie over to a long black car with a chauffeur sitting inside. "What you think about that? You're a star already and you haven't even done anything!" He opened the door, and Willie climbed in the back.

"Mr. Green said for you to drop him off at East End and Seventy-ninth, and then come on back here," Dipsey said to the chauffeur. "Okay?"

The chauffeur touched his hand to his cap and said nothing.

"Hope your mama isn't too mad," said Dipsey. "Give her a kiss from me. We'll knock 'em dead, kid." With that, he smiled a big smile, slammed the door, and was gone.

The long black car moved off through traffic like a whale sliding through the water.

Willie investigated everything in the back seat. There was a telephone, a fold-down bar, and a fur rug on the floor. He craned his neck to see out the windows as the long car glided along.

● ●

Emma was thumping her way along East End heading back to the apartment. The meeting had not been altogether satisfactory from her standpoint. Still, it was only the first meeting. On Wednesday, the brigade would meet, and that would probably be more interesting. She felt a certain lack of stimulation from Saunders, Goldin, and Ketchum. She had wanted to feel close to some people, to feel that she had friends at last, but she didn't feel anything of the kind. She felt as alone and misunderstood as ever.

She tried to think of Saunders in a good light. After all, they had almost the same kind of problem. Their problem related to women's liberation. It was a problem that would be overcome when and if men got any sense.

The person Emma couldn't forgive in this was her mother. How dare her mother sit there and not be aware that her husband was being a male chauvinist pig to her daughter? Didn't she know any better? Even if she just said a few things to him, or even if she had a job; but then, if she had a job, she probably would be a lot more liberated anyway and would have said something to him by now. Or did she really believe that garbage about getting married to a lawyer and having two lovely children?

Emma had a vision of herself as a mother. She saw herself sitting in her room reading a law book. She saw the two lovely children playing in the kitchen, the lovely girl making fudge and the lovely boy bouncing a ball. The lovely boy bounced his ball into the fudge and hot fudge went all over the lovely girl. They both screamed.

The vision fled in disaster. "I'd have to be watching them every minute," said Emma loudly, attracting the attention of a passing hot-dog man, who stopped his cart, thinking she was talking to him.

And the lovely husband! What would he be like? She saw them sitting down in the living room. She saw herself pick up knitting while he picked up his pipe. She watched him orate on his successes of the day. She heard him explain the case he was trying.

He described what a witness had said on the stand.

"But that's hearsay," said Emma. "How could the judge allow that?"

"The judge missed it, Emma," her husband whined. "Why couldn't you?"

She saw his pained face and gave such a shudder of disgust that she set two Yorkies barking in fury. She jumped away from their snapping and started into her apartment house.

Out of the corner of her eye, she saw something she couldn't believe. For a moment she thought it was just another of her fantasies.

No. It was true. She had actually seen Willie getting out of a long, chauffeured car.

She stood waiting for him under the canopy. He saw her and began to run to the elevator. She grabbed him.

"Wait just a minute there. Where do you think you're going? How did you get in that car, and whose car is that?"

"Leggo me!" The elevator opened and Willie dragged her after him into it. The door closed. "Leggo my arm, Emma, you hurting!"

"Not until I get the truth out of you. Where have you been and what have you been doing?"

"I don't have to tell you nothing, nothing in the world! Now, leggo!"

"Come on, you little nit. You want me to blab to your father?"

Willie looked terrified. "I'm not doing anything bad!"

"You want him to know about this?"

"No, but see, it's nothing. I just got a ride home from school in a friend's car."

Emma considered this. It was possible. On the other hand, Willie's left eye was twitching, which it always did when he lied. "You're lying."

"I am not!" yelled Willie, twitching away.

"Listen. I want to tell you something. I could help you a lot, little boy, to get what you want, but if you're going to lie to me—"

"I got what I want!" yelled Willie. Grinning, he ran out of the elevator and down the hall.

"What are you talking about?" called Emma. She lumbered after him. He was through the door and gone by the time she got there. She cornered him in the kitchen. "What's happened?"

Martha said, "Wait a minute! What's going on? We're not having any more fights between you two."

"We're not fighting," said Emma, swinging her book satchel at Willie's head. Willie ducked, snatched two cookies, and fled down the hall, Emma after him.

"You're both late too. What am I supposed to tell your mother?" Martha called after them.

"I'll find out for myself," said Mrs. Sheridan, who erupted from her room just as Willie was slamming the door in Emma's face.

"Where have you been?" she asked Emma.

"I—uh, there's a committee at school—uh, to study—uh, legal problems," said Emma.

"You don't lie very well," said Mrs. Sheridan. "Where have you been?"

"It's the truth," said Emma indignantly, realizing suddenly that it was at least close to the truth. Her mother looked annoyed. "What's the matter?" Emma snarled. "Don't you think girls think about legal problems?"

"That's enough out of you, Emma Sheridan. Go to your room and I don't want to see your face until dinnertime!"

Emma slouched off. Mrs. Sheridan opened the door to Willie's room.

"Now," she said, closing it after her. "Where have you been?"

"Mama!" Willie jumped up and threw his arms around his mother. "I got the best news!"

● ●

Once more in the comfortable confines of her room, Emma confronted her feelings about Willie.

"I honestly don't know if he's worth saving," she said aloud.

"How did he get in that car?" She became aware of the murmur of voices through the wall. Her mother was asking him where he'd been.

He'll probably just lie to her too, the little wretch.

Mothers always believe sons, though, don't they? Emma smiled bitterly to herself. She was of the opinion that Willie looked more like one of those lovely children in her mother's dream world than she did. She didn't look like a lovely anything, and she certainly didn't feel like a child.

On the other hand, she had already brought up Willie's problem to those girls. What did she have to go and do that for? Why couldn't she ever keep her mouth shut? Now they would think she was chicken if she didn't do something.

Her knees shook and everything turned to water again when she thought of her father standing in the living room confronted by a committee.

She tried not to see it, but she had to: she was trying to hate Willie again so she wouldn't have to face this thing.

Well, she thought, so I'm chicken. How do you like that? A black chicken.

She shook with silent laughter.

● ●

"I don't know, dear," said Mrs. Sheridan.

"Oh, Mama, think of it!" Willie's eyes shone.

"Is this summer stock, the one Dipsey was talking about?"

"No, Mama! This is another one that Dipsey's in. He

says he'll take care of me. This one's on Broadway!"

"Broadway?" Mrs. Sheridan looked excited. "You mean that you got a part in a musical on Broadway?"

"Yeah!" Willie did a somersault on his bed. He jumped up and started dancing. "This what I do, Mama, look here!" He danced for her while she watched, her eyes softening.

"Stop that! I'll cut your feet off!" yelled Emma from the other room.

Willie did every step for her, with lots of "And then Dipsey does this," and "Then the music goes like this, so I do this," until he finished the whole thing.

"Why, Willie, I think that's wonderful!" Mrs. Sheridan had her hands clasped together.

She looks as happy as I feel, thought Willie.

"You know, son, your grandfather always wanted to be in a musical, but he never was. I bet if he's looking down from heaven now, he's doing a soft shoe—" Mrs. Sheridan seemed to catch herself. "I don't know what's going to happen. I don't know what your father will say."

"Dipsey said he'll take care of me, Mama, and he said I should tell you that."

"Yes, I'm sure he will. If only there were some way— Is this going to interfere with school?"

"Naw, 'cause the man, the director, Mr. Green, he says school's almost out, and that if I have to come to rehearsals, that they can make some arrangements or something like that. Dipsey asked him."

"If your father didn't have to know until—"

"Yeah, Mama, don't tell him!"

"I don't know, son. That's not right, you know. But it seems, oh, it seems such an opportunity. I think that even he, if he knew that it was Broadway—"

"Mama, please, please, Mama, please don't tell him, please."

"I'll have to think about this, dear, I really will. This is very serious. I want to do the right thing." Mrs. Sheridan was clearly rattled. "I'll have to talk to Dipsey in the morning and get the details."

"Please, Mama," said Willie, looking small.

"I'll see, dear," said Mrs. Sheridan with a worried look on her face. She opened the door and started out. "Wash your hands and face for dinner, dear." She closed the door.

"Yes'm." Willie flung himself on the bed. Oh, boy, how I hate it when they say "I'll see," he thought, then let his mind go back to that dark theater, to that big stage, to the first moment that Dipsey saw it was him, Willie, dancing next to him.

● ●

Willie was grinning so much at dinner he could hardly eat. Emma kept giving him her district-attorney look.

Mrs. Sheridan was nervous as a cat. She spilled water twice and, in an effort to look neither at Willie nor at Mr. Sheridan, stared relentlessly at Emma.

"You have a good day, Willie?" asked Mr. Sheridan jovially.

"I sure did!" crowed Willie. His eyes sparkled. For once, he began to eat what was in front of him without bothering to push it around.

"You play catch with the guys after school?" asked Mr. Sheridan. Mrs. Sheridan knocked over the saltcellar.

Emma wondered anew what image her father had of his son. Willie had never been known to play ball with anyone. Willie didn't even have any friends to play ball with.

"Not exactly," said Willie, grinning again at his mother.

Mr. Sheridan looked to Mrs. Sheridan for an explanation. Mrs. Sheridan said, "Martha, I think you should pass the peas again."

"What peas?" asked Martha. "You wanted peas tonight? All I made was beans."

"I meant the beans," said Mrs. Sheridan. "How silly of me! Isn't it funny how you say one thing and mean another?"

Everyone was looking at her. "I knew perfectly well those were beans and I said peas." She smiled helplessly.

"Happens to everybody," said Mr. Sheridan magnanimously. "Just yesterday, I was in court and I got up to ask the judge for a continuance and I asked for a contempt of court!"

Emma started shaking silently, so hard that the table shook.

Her father smiled at her. "You know what that means?"

Emma nodded, still laughing.

"The judge—it was old Judge Barlow and he's got a pretty good sense of humor—he says, quick as you please, 'If you really want me to cite you for contempt, Counselor, I'll be only too happy.' "

Mr. Sheridan was shaking now too, and Emma noticed that no noise came out of him either when he laughed. "I had barely heard myself, but when he said that, I heard what I had said and you should have seen me stumbling around getting myself out of that one." He shook even harder.

Mrs. Sheridan was laughing too. Willie was smiling.

Emma considered Willie. What was he so happy about? He could only be happy about one thing, because only one thing made him happy. Something must have happened with the dance lessons or with Dipsey. What would that have to do with that long, black car? This was driving her crazy. She'd get him, after dinner, and twist his arm off until he told her.

"Willie and I are going off after dinner for a little while," said Mrs. Sheridan, looking her husband dead in the eye. "It's a new idea I have of each of us spending a little time alone with the kids. I thought I'd take Willie to see a movie, and you and Emma can do something together. Isn't that nice?" Her voice rose shrilly.

Mr. Sheridan looked as though he'd been asked to a cocktail party at the morgue.

"Sure," he said weakly. "I have a little work I brought home, but after that." He gave his wife a steely glare.

"Maybe Emma could help you. She's very good at—" Mrs. Sheridan seemed terrified to continue, because Mr. Sheridan had her eyes in a vise, daring her to say more. ". . . helping," she finished lamely.

"I think I can manage without her," said Mr. Sheridan.

"I have homework," said Emma shortly, wondering that she felt she had to get her father off the hook. She imagined herself picking up the phone and calling Cathy, saying "Emergency" quickly into the receiver and hanging up, rushing to the warehouse, getting a committee together, and coming back to confront her father, because for once he would be alone in the house.

"What movie are you going to?" asked Mr. Sheridan.

"Uh, we haven't picked one yet," said Mrs. Sheridan. "Willie, get the paper and we'll see what's playing."

Willie jumped off his chair with alacrity. Mr. Sheridan continued to stare at Mrs. Sheridan. She refused to look at him and busied herself with her plate, which wasn't easy, as there was nothing on it.

Probably, thought Emma, no one would show up but Ketchum. If my father gets one look at Ketchum, he will bust his sides laughing.

"There's an old Fred Astaire movie on the West Side!" said Willie, coming back with the paper folded to the movie section.

"Typical," said Emma, in spite of herself.

"Isn't there anything else?" asked Mr. Sheridan. "Perhaps," he said with false cheeriness, "you could make it another night."

He hopes that night never comes, thought Emma. He hopes he's never stuck here in the house with me. Well, he'll never see me. I'll go to my room and he'll never know I'm here.

"Look at the ones on Eighty-sixth, dear." Mrs. Sheridan took the paper from Willie. "I don't want to go all the way to the West Side."

"I'm not sure about this, anyway. It'll be awfully late when you come home. Eighty-sixth is no place to be late at night without a man." Mr. Sheridan heaved his shoulders forward.

Even with a man. Emma thought of all the murders on Eighty-sixth they'd read about. What good would a man do? Unless he had a gun. Did her father have a gun?

"Do you have a gun?" she asked.

"Of course not." Mr. Sheridan seemed furious. "I don't believe in guns. That's one reason this country is in the terrible shape it's in, too damned many guns." He seemed about to explode with anger.

"Just asking," said Emma. What a terrific family, she thought. Here's the mother, all gaga to take one kid to the movies, not even asking the other kid if she might like to go. Here's the father, furious that he has to stay at home and might have to talk to his daughter five seconds. Just great. We could go on television. Instead of the Loud Family, we could be the Quiet Family, with nobody talking to anybody from one year to the next. How many families are like this?

She got up from the table, folded her napkin, and said, "So much for the American Family." She clumped out of the room.

"What's the matter, Piggy?" Willie called after her.

"Don't call your sister that." Emma, stopped in the hall, her hands balled into fists, heard Mrs. Sheridan's mild comment. Just wait, Emma said to herself. Just you wait until I get my hands on you, you little bugger. You'll never dance again as long as you live, because you won't have anything to dance *with!*

● ●

When Mrs. Sheridan and Willie were in the elevator going down, Mrs. Sheridan said, "We're going to see Dipsey."

"Oh, no, Mama, we can't. He's working tonight. I

heard the director tell him. He has to be back at the theater tonight. He has to rehearse from eight to ten!"

"Perfect. We'll see him before that." Mrs. Sheridan pulled on her gloves. "You must understand, Willie, I cannot go around lying to your father like this. It'll be just one lie piled on top of another, and I can't do that. I am not a liar."

The door opened. Willie danced along next to her as she walked out of the lobby. The doorman hailed a cab and they got into it.

Mrs. Sheridan gave Dipsey's address, then turned to Willie to explain. "I called Dipsey before dinner. He said he had a rehearsal but that he'd wait for us at the apartment. This won't take long, what I have to tell him."

"What do you have to tell him?" Willie was frantic. "Are you going to tell him that I can't do it?"

"Not necessarily. I'm going to tell him that he is going to have to speak to your father." Mrs. Sheridan was beating her hand against the seat in a mindless, agitated way as she looked out the window.

"But, Mom! Why don't *you* talk to Dad? Dad will do anything you want, and he won't listen to Dipsey. He'll just yell a lot."

"Your father will not 'yell.' Now I don't want to hear any more about this."

Willie sat in silence. His heart hurt. He felt as though his body were made of lead. He slumped down in the seat and stared at the seat ahead of him. There was an advertisement for a musical. His chest felt as though something hateful were sitting on it.

They pulled up in front of the apartment house. Mrs. Sheridan said nothing as they went in, rode in the elevator, and went toward Dipsey's door. At the door she said, "Willie, I want you to let me do the talking. We all know how you feel about this." She rang the bell.

"Hi, Ginny." Dipsey gave his sister a nervous smile. "Ho, Willie. Come in. What's up?"

"As if you didn't know," said Mrs. Sheridan.

Dipsey closed the door behind them. "Wait a minute, Sis. Did Willie tell you that I didn't take him to that audition? It wasn't me that led him by the hand and up on that stage!"

Mrs. Sheridan sat down and kept looking at Dipsey as if she could chop his head off.

"Tell her, Willie!"

"I went myself, Mom. I went myself up on the stage and started doing it."

"He just started right in. I didn't even know he was in the theater. You can't blame me for what he does, now can you?"

"I'm not blaming anybody. Dipsey, don't you understand? This is a child. His father doesn't want him to dance, and now he's got a job in a show. What is his father going to think?"

"Did you tell him?"

"No. I haven't told him, but somebody's got to tell him, and frankly, since you're in this with Willie—I know, I know, you didn't take him there—you're still in it, because you've encouraged him and he followed you to the theater and he did an audition with you. Not me, Dipsey, *you*. For all those reasons, I think you should tell him."

"Boy, people don't change, do they?" Dipsey sat down in an armchair, looking flat, as though everything had suddenly gone out of him. "I don't change and you don't change. You're exactly the way you were as a kid. No matter whose responsibility something was, it was never yours. Listen, Ginny, this is your kid, understand? And that bear over there on East End is your husband, understand? And this is between you and your husband and your kid. Now, why should I tell anybody anything?"

Willie lay back on the couch, wide-eyed, saying nothing, turning his head as each spoke.

"I don't see it that way at all," said Mrs. Sheridan.

"I know you don't, Ginny, and the reason you don't see it that way is that if you saw it that way you'd see that you have to tell him."

"Dipsey, I have not encouraged Willie to dance. I have not gotten us all into this predicament."

"Neither, Sis, have I. And you were wrong not to encourage him. Talent like his *should* be encouraged. And you're wrong not to help him now. He needs you behind him when his father starts yelling at him."

"I am behind him." Mrs. Sheridan looked indignant.

"Yeah, and behind me and behind anybody else you can stand behind, just so you not standing out there in front, getting the punches. I'd like to *see* you stand out in front for a change. I'd like to see you walk in there to that old walrus and say, 'Here's our boy, Willie, and he wants to dance and he's good, and furthermore he's gone and gotten himself a job in a musical, and I want us to back him up and I want you to stop being a jackass.'"

"Dipsey!"

"Aw, come off it, Ginny. You act like you never heard of show business. You act like our family wasn't traveling all their lives from one broken-down old hotel to another. You act like you didn't have a father that was one of the best hoofers this country ever saw, never mind his drinking and never mind he didn't always show up. He was good, he was really *good*. And Willie's good, and what is all this crap, anyway?"

"Dipsey, stop talking like that. All I'm asking you to do is to take the responsibility for having encouraged Willie."

"Woman, you don't know what you're talking about. That husband of yours hates my guts. One word out of me, he'd have me slapped in jail for leading Willie astray. The last person he's going to listen to is me. He's never listened to anything I said yet. He acts like I'm not even in the room. And you expect him to hear me out on this? You got a banana in your ear, lady!"

Willie laughed. His mother frowned at him, and he stopped.

"Am I to understand that you won't help me in this?" Mrs. Sheridan tilted her head back and looked down her nose at Dipsey.

"Hey! This is me, Dipsey. What's got into you?" He imitated her perfectly: "Am I to understand—what kind of talk is that, Sis? You even beginning to talk like that idiot."

"Dipsey!" Mrs. Sheridan nodded her head toward Willie. "Calm down, now. This is the problem. I don't want to lie to him."

"Then tell him! Just walk right in the room and tell him."

"Are you going to help me with this?" Mrs. Sheridan sounded angry now.

"Oh, here it comes. Like I never helped you with anything. Look, Sissy, this is one thing I can't help you with. You got to make up your own mind. You got to decide if you're going to lie or if you're going to go in there and tell him. And this don't have nothing to do with me. Not one thing."

"I'll tell him," said Willie.

Dipsey burst out laughing. "You know, Sis, this little guy has more guts than you've ever heard of. If you had half the guts he's got in his little finger—"

"I don't think that's a good idea, Willie. I think your

father would simply say no."

"Look, Sissy. He's going to say no, any way you look at it. Did you ever think of that? If the Chief Justice of the Supreme Court came in and told him, he'd say no."

Mrs. Sheridan looked down at her purse.

"And you know why he'd say no? Because he ain't going to have anybody run his family but him. That's why. And let me tell you something about yourself that you don't want to look at. You're scared of him. You're scared, Sissy, just plain scared."

Willie turned to his mother in astonishment. "I'm not scared of him, Mama," he said, thinking to himself that he was more scared of Emma than he was of his father.

"Doesn't that embarrass you, Dipsey?" asked Mrs. Sheridan.

"Hell, no, why should I be embarrassed?"

"Willie's seven years old and you're a grown man. You're scared and he's not."

"Honey, I said you the one scared, not me. But so what? You want to act like that, all right. What if I am scared? What's so terrible about that? You think I'm going to have to go prove I'm a man now, by telling him? Sugar, I fell for that jazz a long time ago, but I ain't buying any today. I'm a man and I know it, and a man can be a man and still be scared. I got a damn good reason to be scared of old William. He goes half off his nut when he gets mad. You should have heard him yelling at me over the phone—'Leave my boy alone,' and all this kinda nonsense. I got no time for that crap. Willie got himself a job. Willie wants to keep that job. I hope his parents back him up. But if they don't and Willie loses that job, then you know what I'm going to do? I tell you what I'm going to do. Nothing. That's what. I'll just wait until Willie's older and then Willie will get himself another job or I will help him get a job and then he won't need anybody backing him up, because he'll be old enough to not need you."

"Willie needs you now," said Mrs. Sheridan.

"Ginny, you going to make me mad in a minute. You keep trying, don't you, trying and trying to put this whole thing off on me. Well, it ain't my bag. I didn't have kids because I didn't want to get into just this kind of hassle. You had the kid, not me. Now stick by him."

Dipsey stood up. "I got to go to rehearsal. I think we're just going around in circles now." He leaned over and looked Willie in the eyes. "Willie. I wish I could help you, but believe me, your old man has always hated me, and if I open my mouth, then you can bet your boots you'll never dance in that show. I hope you're going to be dancing next to me. I really do." He touched Willie's head.

"I think the best thing to do, Sis, is for you and Willie to go home now and tell William that Willie wants to be in this show, that it won't interfere with school. We rehearse for six weeks, we don't even go out of town.

By the time we open, Willie will be out of school, so there isn't anything for William to complain about." He got into his jacket. "In fact, I don't know why you tell him anything."

"I can't lie."

"Aw, listen to that. It's not because you can't lie. I don't mean to say that you're a liar, because you're not, but it's not because you can't lie that you're not keeping it secret. It's because you think it will be worse when William finds out, because he's going to be madder than a snake if he thinks you lied to him."

Mrs. Sheridan stood up. "Absolutely not. That's entirely wrong. I feel nothing of the kind. Come on, Willie."

"Don't go away mad," said Dipsey gently.

"Isn't that typical of you. You infuriate somebody, then you turn on that little-boy charm."

Laughing, Dipsey held up his hand to silence her. "Don't start. I'm a rat. You told me for years now how I'm a rat and how every whichaway I'm a rat, and you know what? I think I'm kinda nice. I think maybe you the rat!"

Dipsey ducked as though he were going to be hit, then opened the door for them. "Good to see you, Sis. Bye, Willie Boy. Don't worry. I think maybe everything will come out all right."

How, thought Willie, when nobody will help me?

Mrs. Sheridan didn't even say goodbye. Dipsey came

out, closed and locked his door. He followed behind them to the elevator, pushed the button, then held the door while they got in.

"I have to know soon, you know. I've got to get him to my agent, get him an Equity card. He's been measured already. They think he's going to be in the show."

"Why don't you pick him up after school tomorrow," said Mrs. Sheridan.

"*There* you go." Dipsey looked excited. "I knew you couldn't come from my family without having a little bit of gypsy."

Mrs. Sheridan didn't smile back. They got off the elevator. Mrs. Sheridan hailed a cab before Dipsey could. He held the door for her. "Aw, Ginny," he said softly.

She went right past him into the cab. Willie followed. Willie looked out the window at Dipsey. Dipsey winked at him. The cab drove on toward home.

"Mom?"

"Yes?"

"If you said for him to pick me up after school, then you mean I can do it?"

"We'll see," said Mrs. Sheridan.

There it is again, thought Willie, that *we'll see*. I feel like I'm seeing too much, he thought bitterly. I feel like I'm seeing that Dipsey won't do nothing for me, my mama won't do nothing. I think I'm seeing I got to do it all myself.

He thought fleetingly of Nick the garbage man. He wondered what Nick would do in this situation. Would Nick walk right in and tell Willie's father what was happening? Maybe, if he got mad enough, he would dump garbage all over the living room! The idea sent Willie into fits of giggles.

His mother seemed alarmed. "You're overtired and overstimulated. This has been a big day. You'll go right to bed when we get home."

● ●

By the time Martha had cleaned the kitchen and left, Emma had finished her homework. She devoted her time thereafter to the refrigerator, dividing her attention between pastrami, corned beef, bagels, hard rolls, cream cheese, olives, pickles, and a recent book on children's rights.

She was trying to write a paper for presentation to the Legal Committee of the Children's Army. She had already finished her Children's Bill of Rights, which she planned to present as well. If no other Bill of Rights had been introduced, she planned to push for adoption of hers. The paper she was working on now concerned an idea that had come to her somewhere in the back of her mind when she was having the discussion in the park with Saunders, Goldin, and Ketchum. It had come to her when she realized that she and Saunders were suffering more from a wrong attitude on the part of their respective parents than from anything their parents actually did to them.

She was trying to devise a psychological test to determine parental attitude. She had no idea how the Army would induce parents to take the test, but she reasoned that once they took it, they could be called to account for their attitudes if they were not up to par—in short, if they flunked the test.

She found the book on children's rights, which she had discovered in the library on Saturday, difficult to read. It seemed to go on and on about how there weren't any. Of course, if children didn't have any rights, then naturally it would be hard to write a book about those rights. All you could write about was the absence of them.

She figured that if her test was successful, she would trap her father. He would be exposed as having a rotten attitude. She ate and wrote, ate and wrote, until she had written fifteen pages and eaten three sandwiches, drunk six glasses of chocolate milk, and had four pickles, big ones.

When the door opened, admitting Mrs. Sheridan and Willie, they were talking. She realized that they didn't know she was in the kitchen.

She knew she should call to them, but for some reason, caught as she was with her mouth full and the fridge empty, she chose to say nothing. She didn't move, for fear of making a noise.

"Willie, sit down here a minute." Mrs. Sheridan was almost whispering.

"I know you want to tell your father tonight, but I honestly don't think it would be a good idea."

"I don't want to tell him. I just said I wasn't scared to tell him. You and Dipsey seemed so scared. I don't know why he has to be told, and I don't know why you can't tell him, or you and me tell him together."

Emma sat in the kitchen, not moving, her hand holding a pastrami sandwich, her mouth full, afraid to chew.

"Darling, what I would like to hear you say is that you don't want to go ahead with this. I would like to hear you say that you've given up this whole thing and that you don't care about it any more and that you don't want to have this job in a musical."

Emma dropped the sandwich. She was so shocked that she tried to gasp with her mouth full, and only succeeded in choking. The kitchen was quickly filled with gasping, coughing, wheezing, dropping of books, and other signs of her imminent demise.

Mrs. Sheridan and Willie came running. "It's Emma, she's choking to death!" yelled Willie.

"Look!" he yelled again. "She's turning dark!"

Emma was pushing everybody away, arms flailing. She knew that, although it sounded bad, she was just about to catch her breath. The wheezes died down and she began to breathe again.

"My heavens, darling, what happened?" asked Mrs. Sheridan.

"She was choking, Mama," said Willie.

"Willie!" gasped Emma. "Willie has a job in a musical?"

Too late they heard, as one, the door to the study slam. Mr. Sheridan was already in the kitchen.

"What do you mean, Willie has a job? What is all this yelling about?" He looked like a tornado.

They were too stunned to speak.

"Well, what is it? Don't just stare at me like a bunch of fish. What are you talking about?"

Mrs. Sheridan burst out laughing. "Well, the cat's out of the bag now!" She slapped her hand down on the counter. "It's really funny!"

"What's funny?"

"I'd like to know too," said Emma.

"Emma almost choked to death," said Willie.

"And that's funny?" asked Mr. Sheridan.

"We have a big surprise for you," said Mrs. Sheridan. "Come into the living room. Willie has something to tell you."

She led him away. Willie whispered, "Emma, listen, could you help me?" He was shaking.

"With what?" Emma felt bleary-eyed after her fit.

"I got this job in a Broadway musical. It don't interfere with school. When he hits the ceiling, could you— would you talk good about me?"

Emma stared at him. He had a job in a musical? How good was this kid? "How did you get it?"

"Willie, come in here," called Mrs. Sheridan.

"I walked up on the stage and I danced and they took me."

This kid has guts, thought Emma, before she realized she was thinking about her brother.

"Would you help me, Emma?" His eyes were pleading as he turned to go toward the living room.

"Come on, Willie!"

Willie walked out of the kitchen. Emma sat, picking remnants of pastrami and coleslaw off her book. She slammed the book shut. "How can you get any work done in this family?" she asked the air. She thumped into the living room.

Her father and mother were seated on the couch. Willie was sitting across from them in one of the two armchairs. Emma hovered a bit at the edges of the room, until she finally chose an impartial straight chair against the wall.

"Willie has something to tell us!" said Mrs. Sheridan brightly.

"Mom!" said Willie in an agonized voice.

"Tell what happened this afternoon, dear," said Mrs.

Sheridan, unperturbed. She was holding on to Mr. Sheridan's arm. Mr. Sheridan looked fairly sleepy and exceedingly grumpy.

Willie swallowed. "I went to the Winter Garden Theater, where Dipsey was in rehearsals—"

"You did what?" Mr. Sheridan sat up straight, untangling himself from his wife and putting a hand on each knee.

Willie swallowed again. "I went over to the Winter Garden Theater—"

"And just where is this Winter Garden?"

"Broadway and Fiftieth." Willie said this so low he could barely be heard.

"You mean to tell me that you went all the way from your school—I presume you went to school, did you not?"

Willie nodded, petrified.

"You went all the way from your school to Fiftieth and Broadway, even after having been told that you were not to go across town by yourself, were not, in fact, to go anywhere but school and then straight home?"

Willie nodded again.

Emma looked at Willie's legs. He was shaking so hard he seemed to be dancing with his knees.

"In other words, you performed an act of deliberate disobedience?"

Mrs. Sheridan said, "Let him tell the story."

Mr. Sheridan obviously didn't take to the idea, but

he went along with it. "What did you do there?"

Something's missing, thought Emma, something important.

"I went in the theater. It was dark. I sat in one of the back rows."

"Speak up. You can't be heard!" said Mr. Sheridan.

Emma mentally finished his sentence, "You can't be heard in the courtroom," and realized, suddenly, what was missing. Of course! Here was a prosecutor in the form of her father, here was a suspected criminal in Willie, here was even a judge in the shape of her mother, but where was the defense lawyer? Willie had no one defending him!

"I sat in one of the back rows. These men were talking down front, and they were saying some boys were going to audition with Dipsey."

"Oh, they did, did they? And I suppose you thought you'd show them what you could do with some fancy stepping, right?" Mr. Sheridan was sneering.

"Objection!" said Emma. Every head turned in her direction. "Prosecutor is badgering the witness."

Her father looked as though the chair had spoken. "What is this? What do we have to hear from this one for? Isn't one rotten apple enough?"

"Pay no attention, dear," said Mrs. Sheridan, grabbing his arm again and making him lean back on the couch. "Come on, Willie, tell us about it. Don't be afraid."

"Dipsey came out and he did the number I've been practicing—"

"Oh-ho! So you've been working up a number, have you? Well, fine, that's just fine. You don't pay a damned bit of attention to what your father says, do you?"

"Let him tell it, dear."

Willie was so rattled he kept bobbing up and down in his chair like a swimmer coming up for air. "This kid comes out and dances with Dipsey—"

"Fine. So they have somebody. Why didn't you come home?"

"This kid was terrible, Dad!" This was the first display of temper on Willie's part.

"So what! Let his family worry about what happens to him in ten years. You get your ass home after school!"

"Objection!" said Emma. "The District Attorney is leading the witness."

"Leading him where?" asked Mr. Sheridan.

"Home from school," said Emma.

"Leading the witness doesn't mean that. When you don't know what you're talking about, you'd better keep your mouth shut!"

"May I remind the District Attorney that if he would question the witness fairly, he might find out what *he* was talking about."

"Get her out of here!" Mr. Sheridan stood up. Mrs. Sheridan grabbed at his arm.

"Sit down, William. I want Willie to tell you what happened."

Willie looked queasily at Emma. He wasn't sure what she was talking about, so he wasn't sure if she was on his side or not.

"What is this nonsense?" Mr. Sheridan looked at his wife in desperation. "Can't you handle these kids any better than this? One of them running all over town all the time, and the other one running off at the mouth!"

Emma's mind was racing ahead. How could she prepare a case for the defense when she hadn't heard the whole story? Before she knew it, she was on her feet. "May it please the court, I would like a few minutes to confer with my client."

"That does it!" said Mr. Sheridan, standing again. "What in the name of God is going on here?"

"I am simply begging the indulgence of the court for a few minutes of time to confer with my client on matters pertinent to this case."

"It takes your breath away," said Mr. Sheridan. He sat down, muttering, "If I'd ever talked to my father that way, he'd have slit my throat."

Emma ignored him. She marched over to Willie, who thought she was going to beat him up. She grabbed his arm. "Into the kitchen a minute," she said. He went with her.

"Now, I'm going to try to help you," she whispered. "But you have to tell me the truth."

"This is the truth," said Willie.

"What is the truth? What happened?"

"I went in there like I said. This nutsy kid comes out and does the number real bad. I mean, Emma, it was *bad*. So, next time Dipsey starts, I know some other kid is going to run out, because it's the same music, so I run up on the stage instead, even before Dipsey knows I'm there, and I do the number with him!"

"Why didn't you tell anyone you had been practicing something?"

"He would have stopped it, you know that. What a dumb question."

"Is that why you didn't tell anyone your whereabouts on the afternoon in question?"

"My where-a-who?"

"Is that why you didn't tell anyone where you were going when you went to the theater?"

"Sure. He wouldn't have let me!" Willie began to doubt that Emma was sane.

"After you did your dance, what happened?"

"I got the job!" said Willie, breaking into an enormous grin.

"And you want, naturally, to be able to do it."

She was definitely insane, Willie concluded. Of course he wanted the job.

"Will you have to leave school?"

"Listen, in there. Stop getting your stories straight. I don't have all night, and I have to get up early." Mr. Sheridan sounded a bit more jovial.

Willie shook his head. "Rehearsals are after school, and I'll be out for the summer before the show starts."

Emma took him back into the living room and sat him down on his chair.

"May it please the court," said Emma, standing in the middle of the room and facing her father and mother. "I would like to plead a mistrial on the basis of the fact that in this case the complainant, Mr. William Sheridan, Sr., happens also to be the District Attorney."

"Listen, smart-ass." Mr. Sheridan pointed a finger at her. "You think you know so much. I'll have you in contempt of court in three minutes."

"—and is also the judge. My client, William Sheridan, Jr., has, therefore, no possibility of a fair trial."

"But you have a very good possibility of getting your ass whacked," said Mr. Sheridan. "Now, sit down and shut up."

"I'll stand."

"All right, Willie. Since you have a loyal sister who seems to feel your rights to a fair trial are being prejudiced, I will begin again, calmly, to try to find out what you did on the afternoon of the second; that is, today."

Willie had his thumb in his mouth, having fled back into his youth.

"Sit up," said Emma. "Make a more pleasing appearance for the jury." Willie looked around for the jury.

"Finish your story, Willie," said his father.

"I watched this boy dance with Dipsey and he was real bad. He couldn't do it half as good as I could. So when Dipsey come to start again, I went up on the stage and did it with him."

"Son, you must have practiced this many times. You must therefore have disobeyed me many times. Did you not know that you were being bad?"

"Objection. My client could not be honest about this situation because he would have been incarcerated."

"Emma, get out of the way!" Mr. Sheridan bellowed.

"Willie, dear, what your father wants to know is whether you knew you were being disobedient. Did you, dear?"

"My client takes the Fifth Amendment," said Emma quickly.

"Will you tell your daughter to shut up?" asked Mr. Sheridan patiently.

"Emma, please, wait a minute until we are finished with Willie."

Emma didn't even hear her mother, so lost was she in her courtroom activities. All she heard was a sort of buzz running through the crowd filling the courtroom at Foley Square, in the middle of which she stood in a Bella Abzug hat.

"This boy is innocent until proven guilty by due

process!'' she fired back at her father.

"I knew I was bad, but I had to do it!'' said Willie.

Emma hit her forehead with her hand. "Shut up, you nincompoop! How can I defend you when you insist on hanging yourself? May it please the court, I request a recess.''

"Well now, son, if you knew you were bad, why did you do it?''

"Objection! Counsel is intimidating the witness!''

"I had to because I had to get that job,'' said Willie.

"Job?'' Mr. Sheridan looked thoroughly confused.

"I got it, Daddy! I got the job!'' Willie was grinning again.

"Don't volunteer information!'' said Emma, clearly at the end of her tether.

"Let me get this straight. You say, son, that you have a job?''

"Yeah!'' Willie was beaming. "I got a job in a musical!''

"You do, really?'' asked Emma.

"He really does!'' said Mrs. Sheridan, smiling, to Mr. Sheridan.

"Where is that Dipsey?'' Mr. Sheridan got up. "He'll never see the light of day when I get through with him!''

"Dipsey didn't do it!'' said Willie loudly. "I did! I did it all by myself!''

"Stop saying that,'' said Emma. "You could plead undue influence.''

"This will all be over by tomorrow afternoon," said Mr. Sheridan. "I'll get in touch with whoever is producing this musical and tell him that a mistake has been made." He stood over Willie. "A very big mistake," he said slowly.

"Under the Constitution," said Emma, clearing her throat, "he has a right to the pursuit of happiness."

"I'll constitution you right out of this room," said Mr. Sheridan, looking steadily at Emma. Then he said, "Sit down, Emma."

It was the way he said it. Emma herself couldn't figure out how he had said it, how anybody could say anything that would make her sit down instantly, but whatever he had done, it worked. She sat down.

There was a change in everyone. Everyone waited for Mr. Sheridan to speak. Willie stopped wiggling his feet and sat still, looking up timorously at his father.

"I want to speak frankly to you people. I want to pretend, and to have you pretend, for the moment, that I am not a father and a husband, that I am just a man." He looked around at them. He took a stance that Emma recognized as the one he took when addressing the jury (the one and only time she had even seen him in a courtroom), one hand resting on his hip, the other gesturing with his glasses.

"What kind of man is this in front of you? Let me tell you a little bit about him." He rocked back on his heels, then forward again. "He grew up on the toughest street in Bedford-Stuyvesant. He worked from the time he was nine years old, but he didn't bring his money home to his mother because he didn't have any mother at home. He didn't have any father at home either."

Oh, God, thought Emma, it's choke-up time. Now we're going to hear how sad his life was and how wonderful ours is and how wonderful he is as a father.

"The money he earned went to feed himself and his younger brother. His father appeared every now and then and stole whatever this boy could manage to save after the room rent and some food. This man standing before you went to the library every day and he read. This man made straight A's in school. He graduated from high school. This man worked while he went through City College, while he went through law school. This man has worked every day of his life since he was nine years old. This man was spit on every day of his life in one way or the other for being black." Mr. Sheridan seemed to lose control of himself. He sputtered. "I was treated like an animal." The words seemed to rip from his mouth, hurting him as they came through. "What you can't understand, you two kids who have always been clean and fed, is that I *felt* like an animal."

Emma's sympathy careened toward her father. She had felt like an animal, sometimes at school like a strange animal and always, upon looking in the mirror, like a fat animal. She had never thought of her father as *feeling* anything and she searched his face for signs of more.

She watched him shake himself and get control. He resumed his speech.

"This man meets and rescues, yes, rescues, this woman, your mother, from a life of hardship and pain, heartbreak and sorrow because she was the daughter of a"—he sneered the word, looking straight at Willie—"dancer. This so-called dancer was a man who didn't want to work for a living. I supported this so-called dancer for the rest of his life, until he died a broken-down drunk." He paused to let this sink in.

"This man you see in front of you is now in middle age. This man fought to get his brother out of a slum, this man fought to rescue his wife from insecurity, this man is fighting today to keep all three of you living here in a clean place, going to private schools, wearing nice clothes, having a nice warm home to come back to at night with a good hot meal at the end of the day." He stopped and looked at them all.

"This man is not going to stop doing this. This man is not going to let anyone else stop him from doing this." He pointed to Willie. "This boy is going to continue to go to school, to come home to a nice home, to grow up straight with nobody laughing at him and calling him names. He will go to college. He will have a profession which is worthy of the name 'profession.' Nobody is going to stop me from seeing that this boy gets what he deserves in this world." He stopped and looked at Willie a long time.

"Son," he said finally. "We do not understand each other very well at this moment, but in the future I know that will change. I want you to listen to what I have to tell you now."

Willie's eyes were huge. Mr. Sheridan regarded him steadily.

"You will do what I say now, even though you don't agree with it and even though you don't understand it, because you will have faith that I can see further into your future than you can. You will continue to go to school and you will stop all this ridiculous talk about musicals. I will straighten out this situation you've gotten yourself into. By tomorrow it will be all over. There is to be no recurrence of this, do you understand?"

Willie stared, his mouth hanging open. Mr. Sheridan turned and walked heavily out of the room.

Swell, thought Emma. She had a vision of her father wearing the headdress of a gypsy fortune-teller and looking further into their futures than they could, into Willie's future, anyway. He hadn't mentioned any future for her. She didn't have a future.

"Don't feel too badly, Willie," purred Mrs. Sheridan.

Looking at Willie, Emma could see that it was not a question of feeling badly. It was not a question of feeling at all. Willie was totally defeated. He was a limp doll. He didn't sit in the chair, he hung in it, his head rolled to one side as though he didn't have the strength or the amount of caring it took to hold it up. He looked as though he would never care about anything in the whole world again.

"You mustn't be so sad about it," Mrs. Sheridan went on. "You'll understand when you're older, and perhaps not that much older either. Perhaps when you're fifteen or sixteen you'll be old enough and your father will feel differently. It's not as though this were the only job in a musical you'll ever be offered."

Something about this last remark created a change in Willie. He sat up straight. "I'm doing to do it," he said. He stood up. "I don't care what you say, I'm going to do it!"

He ran toward the front door. Mrs. Sheridan gasped. He ran out into the hall.

Only Emma realized what was happening. She ran after him. She grabbed him just as the elevator door was opening.

"Oh, no, you don't," she said, holding him as he struggled.

"Leggo me! I got to go! I got to get out of here!" Willie was yelling. Emma dragged him back toward the apartment. Mrs. Sheridan was coming down the hall.

Willie was hysterical, screaming and crying at the top of his lungs. "Leggo! Leggo! You all hate me. Nobody cares what happens to me! I got to do it myself! Leggo me, *let go*, Emma!"

Mr. Sheridan appeared in the doorway. Emma was almost up to the door, dragging Willie.

"Give him to me," said Mr. Sheridan.

"No, Emma, don't let him!" Willie was a mess, bawling, crying, and drooling.

Mr. Sheridan pulled Emma's arms away and picked Willie up like a handkerchief. He was back inside the apartment before Emma or Mrs. Sheridan moved.

Emma ran back into the apartment. Mrs. Sheridan followed and closed the door.

Willie was still screaming. He was furious and miserable, punching out at his father's face as his father held him at arm's length.

"You bastid!" Willie shouted. "You don't understand anything. You never think about nobody but yourself. I'll kill you!"

Mrs. Sheridan looked terrified. Mr. Sheridan looked angry and puzzled at the same time. He still held Willie away from him, as one would hold an angry alley cat determined to scratch.

Willie landed his fist next to Mr. Sheridan's nose. Mr. Sheridan said, "You're hysterical," and gave Willie a slap across the face.

Willie dissolved into a bath of tears.

"Stop that!" yelled Emma. "Stop hitting him! You can go to jail for that, and besides, he's right. You never think about anybody else." God knows, you don't think about me, she thought. God knows.

Willie fell down into a little pile next to the couch.

"You never think about anybody, but just how you think they should live. You don't even know us! You don't know what we think!" Emma was livid. She didn't even know what she was saying, she was so angry.

Mr. Sheridan was looking at her in surprise.

"You just stand up here and tell us what your life was like! Who cares? You don't care what our lives are like!"

"Emma! Stop it," Mrs. Sheridan said anxiously. "You don't know what you're saying!"

"I do too know what I'm saying! And as for you, what are you but a fink? You go right along with whatever he says, and you think everything he does is wonderful, even all his dumb talking about what kind of hard time he had as a kid. What about the hard time we have? Just because we aren't starving doesn't mean everything is great. That's what *he* thinks. We get a nice hot meal at night. Is that it? Is that all we get? Is that all life is about?"

"When you don't have it," said Mr. Sheridan steadily, "you're damned right, that's what life is all about. You're so fat and spoiled you wouldn't know what life is about if it came up and hit you in the face!"

The word *fat* went through Emma like an ice pick. "Spoiled! That's a word you made up to make yourself feel better. What am I spoiled for? You mean because I don't think you're wonderful, because I don't wallow all over the floor after your stupid speech about your life and say, 'Daddy, Daddy, you're wonderful.' Well, you know why, don't you? Because I've heard that damn speech five thousand times, and I'm sick of hearing it."

"Shut up," said Mr. Sheridan.

Emma couldn't believe the hatred she saw in his eyes. He's looking at me like that, she said to herself, that hate is for me.

Her knees began to shake and all courage deserted her. "It doesn't make any difference anyway, your speech, because what has that got to do with us? You never even look at us!" She tried, but her voice shook and she knew she was finished. She knew the look of hatred would be forever in her mind, that nothing would ever take it away. She knew that it was all proven now, all the thoughts she'd had, all the guesses she had guessed about his hating her. It was true. He hated her.

"Shut up and go to your room," he said, his eyes the same.

"Don't leave, Emma!" screamed Willie. "Don't leave me here!"

"I'm not going to leave my brother," said Emma, looking at her father with the same hatred he'd given her.

A memory came over Emma, suddenly, of her father the way he had been before Willie was born. In those days he had taken her downtown with him, sometimes, way downtown to his office. He'd held her up to let her look out the big windows at the people, small as toys, and at the boats on the river. That was before he talked about nothing but *my boy* this and *my boy* that, after Willie was born.

"I don't know what's wrong with you, little girl," her father said heavily, "but you got a lot of problems. Look at her," he said to Mrs. Sheridan. "Look at the way she's looking at me."

Emma turned her back on him.

Willie thought she was leaving. "Emma!" he screamed.

She stood there with her back to her parents. "I'm not going anywhere. Come to my room with me."

Willie scrambled toward her across the floor.

"Hold it," said Mr. Sheridan. "This family is going to talk. We are going to sit right down here in this room and I don't care if it takes all night. We are going to understand what is going on here."

"I'll tell you what's going on," said Willie, clinging to Emma's leg, "you being a bastid, that's what's going on."

"Stop using that word, right now!" said Mrs. Sheridan.

"Mama, go make me a pot of coffee, will you, and see if there's some ice cream in there for the kids." Mr. Sheridan spoke gently to his wife. She hurried to the kitchen.

He sat back on the couch and put his legs up on the footstool. He looked tired. He examined the ceiling thoughtfully, then brought his gaze down slowly, very slowly, until it fastened on Willie and Emma. They watched.

"You kids sit down over there."

"Willie," said Emma, "you don't have to answer anything and you have the right to have a lawyer present."

Mrs. Sheridan came back in. "I put the coffee on." She handed a dish of ice cream to each child.

"Now that you've informed Willie of his rights," said Mr. Sheridan to Emma, "I want to remind you that I am not arresting him. I want all four of us to sit down here and have a conversation, that's all."

Emma and Willie ate ice cream, saying nothing, not looking at him.

"You sit down too," he said to Mrs. Sheridan.

"Now," he said, unbuttoning his vest, "this family seems to have quite a few misunderstandings going on here."

Quite a word to describe hatred, thought Emma. I know hatred when I see it, and nothing he's going to say is going to make any difference.

"First of all, I gather I've been boring Emma with stories of my life."

"Oh, she didn't mean that!" said Mrs. Sheridan.

"Oh, yes, she did."

I'll give him that, thought Emma, he's right on that one.

"She meant it. She doesn't like hearing that her father had a hard life."

Willie and Emma sat eating dutifully, looking down into their bowls.

"Second, she thinks her life is just as hard, maybe even harder, right, Emma?"

Emma didn't answer, didn't look up.

"And I gather my son here thinks I'm ruining his life."

Willie said nothing, just kept eating ice cream.

He doesn't even *like* ice cream, thought Emma. He's just doing that to have something to do so he won't have to look at Dad. I told him to keep his mouth shut and he is.

She took courage from this. She decided to keep her mouth shut too. What would their father do confronted by silence? What could he do?

Unless he puts us on a rack, she thought, and tears out our toenails, there's no way he can make us talk. She decided to let him rave on.

"I gather," he continued, "that I am regarded, by this family, as the worst excuse for a father the world has ever seen."

Emma recognized, and noted, the lawyer's technique of exaggeration.

"I gather that you two, at least, would like to have nothing more to do with this poor excuse for a father."

Emma realized what he was doing. He wanted to be corrected. He wanted somebody to jump up and say, "Oh, no, Daddy, we love you."

"Oh, no, dear," said Mrs. Sheridan, "I don't think they mean that at all."

There she goes, the jack-in-the-box. Emma watched her mother with contempt. How could she fall for such a stupid thing? How could she constantly reassure this man that he was an okay person, when he wasn't, he wasn't at all. He didn't know what he was talking about half the time, yet up she'd pop, still agreeing with him. Could it be that she was dumb?

She'd never thought about this. She'd never thought about either of her parents being dumb or smart, but just there in some way, like the sun was there, or a rock, or the sky. Her father couldn't be that dumb, she reasoned, because he was a lawyer. But what about her mother?

It was hard to think about her mother at all. Something hurt inside her when she tried to think about her mother. There were things she never wanted to ask her mother. There were answers she never wanted to hear. It was one thing to think about her father hating her. She hated him too, but she never wanted to know what her mother thought of her. She'd just as soon never find out about that.

"All right," said Mr. Sheridan. "You've finished that

ice cream. You can stop looking in those bowls. You can look up here at me and tell me what all this is about."

Willie and Emma kept looking down.

"Got that coffee ready, Mama?"

"Yes, dear."

Mrs. Sheridan came back into the room with a mug from which steam rose. "It's past Willie's bedtime, dear."

To hear her, thought Emma, you'd think there was nothing happening at all.

Mr. Sheridan took a sip of coffee. "Mmm, that's good, good hot strong coffee. You always did make great coffee." He smiled at his wife and she smiled back at him.

Emma sneered. Look at that, she said to herself, look at them smiling at each other. Look at my mother, happy for a pat, like a good dog. Look at my father, thinking about coffee at a time like this, always thinking about his stomach.

"You can stop staring at your feet now, both of you." Mr. Sheridan sounded almost cheery now. "The big bad wolf isn't going to eat you up."

Emma groaned. She couldn't help herself.

"What's that for?" he asked. "Am I boring you again?"

Now she was in for it. She never should have uttered a sound. She decided she would make her speech on Willie's behalf, then get up and go to bed. Tomorrow she would organize a committee to come and talk to her father.

"I don't think you understand," she began calmly, "that Willie cares a great deal about this musical and about dancing in general. I mean that he is going to be a dancer and that nothing you can do or say is going to change that. You can't stop him. If he has to wait until he's grown, he'll still do it. I don't think you see that."

Mr. Sheridan had obviously not seen it. He blinked his eyes. "I don't think, Emma, that you know very much about seven-year-olds. They don't always want to do what they think they want to do at seven. For instance, when you were seven, you wanted to be a shoplifter."

Emma's eyebrows flew up. "What?"

"You sat down and told me very seriously that you had seen a shoplifter on television and that you didn't understand what was wrong with that because all those things were out there for people to take and so why was this lady arrested when she took something. Furthermore, you thought you'd be a shoplifter when you grew up, because the lady had gotten a lot of nice things."

Emma was mortified. Her mother and father were laughing. Willie was looking up at her with sleepy, surprised eyes. She sat, her hands holding her ice-cream bowl, watching her mother and father laugh. It was not only not funny, it wasn't fair, bringing up something one had done when one was seven. She didn't think he'd proved his point, either.

"I may yet be a shoplifter," said Emma, and stood up. She loved watching their faces fall. "I'm going to bed now and Willie is going with me." She took Willie's hand and together they left the room and marched down the hall. There, she thought, see how they like being talked to the way they talk to us, see how they like a taste of their own medicine.

At Willie's door, she stopped. "Willie, go to sleep. If either one of them comes in and tries to talk to you alone, then you yell for me and come into my room and get me if I'm asleep. Tomorrow I'm going to do something. You're going to keep that job, so go to sleep and don't think about anything."

Willie smiled. "Thanks," he said simply. "What are you going to do?"

"Don't worry. Just believe me. It's going to work out."

"Okay. Good night."

"Good night."

He went into his room. Emma walked down the hall. She could hear her mother and father muttering to each other in the living room, but she didn't even care what they were saying.

• •

Emma lurked around the front of the luncheonette for five minutes, peering through the foggy window at Harrison Carter's Adam's apple making swift movements up and down as he drank his Coke.

She finally propelled herself through the door, feeling like the lead in a spy movie.

His greeting, a brief nod, did nothing to dispel this illusion.

"Sheridan, isn't it?" He nodded, jerking his long red head convulsively. He did look like a flamingo. His acne was fierce. His eyes, behind his glasses, looked like raisins.

It took her less time to explain the situation than she had thought it would. What seemed so complicated to her was evidently second nature to him. All the small details which seemed so interesting to her were dismissed by him. He got the point quickly. Emma was, evidently, not the first one to bring it up.

"We can't help you," he said shortly.

"Why? I thought that's what this Children's Army was for!"

"No." He sighed. "I seem to spend half my time explaining this. Unless a child is actually being damaged for life, we can't intervene."

"But . . . can't you see that this attitude toward Willie would be damaging to him?"

"Yes. Of course, I can see that. Look at it this way: if your father were planning to have his feet amputated, we'd do something."

"Oh, swell."

"Or even if he were kicking Willie around. But he's not. He's simply saying he doesn't think it's a good idea for his son to be taking dancing lessons. And"—Harrison Carter took a deep breath—"I'm not sure I don't agree with him."

Emma's mouth fell open.

"Now, before you call me a male chauvinist pig, let me explain. I don't know how it happened, but it seems as though your brother is off on the wrong foot. He seems to be identifying with his mother, not his father. I can understand, therefore, that his father might want to stop this and get him back on the right track."

"You'd have to know Willie," said Emma. She felt tired. This wasn't getting anywhere at all. She was, in fact, beginning to dislike Harrison Carter. He seemed to have everything wrapped up.

"What do you do?" she asked. "Just take nice safe cases you know you can win?"

He frowned, looking down into his Coke. "You know, Sheridan, we've handled some very difficult situations. You haven't been with us long—"

"So far, nothing applies," Emma interrupted.

"What do you mean?"

"So far, nothing that's bothering me or my friends

can be handled by the Army, that's what."

"The Army is always open to complaints. I'm always ready to listen to grievances." Harrison Carter's glasses seemed to grow thicker.

"Everything that's bothering us has to do with parental attitudes toward us. I mean, nobody is actually doing anything to us, but they're just ruining us, that's all."

"How?"

"By the way they think about us. It's the way they *see* us. After a while you can't help it, you start to see yourself that way."

"Oh. You mean, if your father keeps acting like you're a thief, you finally steal?"

"Sort of." Emma felt that, in some subtle way, she was losing ground. She found herself wishing her father had belted her once, then it would be simple.

Harrison Carter nodded shortly, as though now he understood the problem. This seemed to please him, reinforce him in some way.

"I'm afraid you've misunderstood the purpose, the most valid purpose of the Children's Army, and that is the question of children's rights. The Army is devoted, primarily, to the study of children's rights. The purpose of the complaints being filed and committees handling those complaints is primarily for the education of the membership. Naturally, pressing cases, which are the only kind we handle, are also helped, but the main purpose is not so much to help individuals as it is to impress upon the membership that children have no rights under our legal system. I mean, you understand, don't you, that your father actually owns you, like a slave?"

Emma nodded. She had thought of that, but not in exactly those terms. "He can't sell me, though. Remember that dope addict that tried to sell his baby on the subway?"

"Yes. As a matter of fact, we're looking into that. I think we may move on that. Now, there is a serious case."

Humiliating, thought Emma. My case isn't serious enough. I guess I sound like one of those kids who wants her wallpaper changed. "What does Willie have to do? Come out in a dress for you to see this is serious?" she snapped back at him.

Harrison Carter looked shocked, but recovered quickly. "If, for example, your father were dressing him or forcing him to dress in girl's clothes, we would handle that."

Emma felt totally frustrated. As usual when she felt like that, she attacked. "By the way, I have a serious complaint about the name of this organization."

"Oh?"

"Yes. I see no reason for it to be called an army. We have no guns, we have no plans to attack anyone—"

"We don't?"

"Do we?" She wondered, suddenly, how much of this group was submerged like an iceberg. Was all that she had seen only the tip?

"You see your reaction?" asked Harrison Carter. "That's exactly why we are called the Children's Army, because, if and when we are ever discovered by adults, or by the police, then at least we have the advantage of instilling fear into their hearts. People will be afraid of something called the Children's Army."

"What good will that do? If they get afraid, they'll really squash us!"

Harrison Carter smiled. "I don't think you need to worry about that." He smiled again.

She realized that it was a condescending smile. "Why not?"

"Well, first of all, you're a girl."

"So?" Emma felt a sinking feeling. Here it comes. They're all alike.

"If we're attacked, we'll mobilize. That is, the boys—"

"Oh, I see. You guys will handle the situation."

"Something like that." He seemed to want to change the subject.

"Where are you training all these midget John Waynes?" Emma was furious. They had lied. They had said there was no violence involved. Training for future violence was certainly violence.

"Listen, Sheridan, we've gotten off the subject here. I'd like you to understand that we would like to help your brother, but at the moment we can't. If things get worse, we can discuss it again. You see, if we went in there now, your father would throw us out, and he'd be right. He's just raising his kid the way he sees fit, and that's his legal right. Besides, he's a lawyer, he'd get suspicious, he might even investigate, he might find out things. He might blow everything up in our faces."

"You're chicken, aren't you?"

"If that's all you want to talk about, Sheridan, I think we'll break up this meeting now." Harrison Carter took a loud slurp of his Coke and got up. He pulled his jacket around him and went out the door, never looking back.

Emma ordered a hamburger. When it was put down in front of her, she ordered another. She ate steadily through the first and through the second.

The situation, she said to herself, is impossible. My father controls my life. He controls Willie's life. I am only fighting for Willie because I want to fight for myself.

She let this last thought fly through her mind like a southbound goose, not really hearing herself think it.

When it gets right down to it, the Children's Army is no different from any adult organization. Males were in control and would depend upon force. Did they really think they were going to have a war with adults? She had a vision of Harrison Carter in a uniform on a salt flat in Jersey somewhere, saluting and goose-stepping in front of a bunch of three-year-olds.

"Ridiculous," she said aloud, then remembered where she was. She ordered another chocolate milk.

Whatever the Children's Army was or wasn't, it was not going to help her now. That was clear.

Where did things stand?

This afternoon Willie was being allowed to go to rehearsal. He had told Emma at breakfast that their mother had told Dipsey to pick him up after school. Emma had gotten Willie out of the house before Mrs. Sheridan could change her mind.

My father will find out about it tonight. It's a good thing I ate something, she said to herself as she got up to leave. God knows what dinner will be like.

● ●

The minute Emma walked in the door, she knew something was very different.

For one thing, her father was sitting in the living room looking out at the river. He did not see her when she came in. Her father never sat in the living room until after dinner.

For another, her mother was sitting in the living room too. "Hello, dear. You're late."

"I went to get a Coke," said Emma. Her father did not turn his head.

"Did you eat anything?"

"I saw some great-looking hamburgers," said Emma, hedging. She hated to lie and wouldn't, unless her back was pushed to the wall.

"Well, I'm glad you didn't eat any, because we're having pot roast for dinner. Why don't you go to your room now, dear? You must have some homework to do."

Emma looked from her mother to the still-silent figure of her father. What was happening?

"Okay." She started back toward the hall. "Is Willie home?"

Her father moved almost imperceptibly, nothing much, just a slight gesture of the shoulders.

"Not yet, dear," said her mother with a forced gaiety. "I'm sure he'll be here soon." Her mother glanced at her in a way that was almost pleading. She seemed to be asking Emma not to ask any more questions. "I'll call you for dinner," she said sweetly.

Emma went down the hall. The kitchen door was closed. She could hear Martha inside. She reasoned that the door was closed to allow Mr. and Mrs. Sheridan to talk without being overheard. Or were they waiting to pounce on Willie when he came in?

She wanted desperately to listen. She went down the hall to her room, opened the door, and put her books on the desk. If she were caught, there would be hell to pay.

She had to know what they were planning to do to Willie. She crept down the carpeted hall until she was right next to the living-room door.

"It's not that, Ginny, not that at all. It's the loss of respect that I am going to suffer. You've countermanded my order, don't you see? It's you who's the father, in Willie's mind."

How can my mother be my father? thought Emma. Is he nuts?

"That is not so," said Mrs. Sheridan in a voice that was stronger than any Emma had ever heard her use. "We are two people. I think one thing. You think another. We disagree with each other. I do not think this will harm Willie, and I do think it will do a great deal for him. If he's got something going for him that is exclusively his, the way dancing is, I think he'll feel better about himself and I think he will do better in school."

"Wait till the first guy finds out about it, just wait till Willie comes home from school all beaten up because some guy has called him a faggot."

"Oh, honey. I don't think that's going to happen. That might have happened in your day, but kids aren't that way now. Even Dipsey wasn't beaten up. I think you're exaggerating this."

"Look, Ginny, I'm a man and I understand men. I understand boys too. If you buck me in this, you're going to make Willie lose respect for me. He's going to think that women are the strong ones, that all he has to do is run to his mama and cry a little and he'll get what he wants. You're not going to make a man of him. Don't you see that?"

"No. I don't see that. I think Willie will grow up to be a man because he's a little boy. I don't think you have to take the only thing he loves away from him to make him grow up a man."

Emma's eyes widened in surprise. Her mother was absolutely right. Willie was a little boy, so how could he grow up to be anything else but a man?

There was silence in the living room. The next time her father spoke, Emma could hear in his voice that the expression in his eyes was cold.

"Do you plan to continue this, Virginia?"

He had to be furious. He never called her mother by her full name.

There was a long pause before her mother said, "Yes. I have to. I have to do what I think is right."

There was silence then. Emma heard Martha coming toward the kitchen door. If she came out to set the table, she'd run smack into Emma crouched there.

Emma stole back toward her room. She went in, closed the door, and sank into her old chair.

She was thunderstruck. Her mother was standing up to her father. It wasn't like her mother at all. What had made her change? Emma had always thought of her mother as being too frightened to disagree, much less to stand up for what she believed in.

The strangest thing of all seemed to be that her father was taking it. He wasn't yelling, or bellowing orders, or making speeches about himself. He was just sitting in a chair looking at the river with a defeated look on his face.

She wondered if her father felt he was wrong or if he felt that somebody had gotten the better of him.

A curious feeling began to snake its way up to Emma's consciousness. It was a feeling she didn't remember ever having before. It curled softly around the edges of her brain. She felt a torpid reluctance to let it in.

What she was feeling burst through to her. I've done this, she thought. I've beaten him.

Shame overtook her. She felt lost. She was rolling around in an area where every feeling was unfamiliar.

What am I talking about? She tried to get hold of herself, sat up in the chair, shook herself like a wet dog to ward off a flood of feeling.

My mother has stood up to him. *She* has done this, not me. In her heart, Emma knew this was a lie. She, Emma, had wanted to beat her father for so long and she had wanted it so hard that now she didn't know what to feel. Now that he was beaten, it didn't matter who had done it, but only that it was done and that she didn't feel what she thought she would feel.

She thought of all the times he had beaten her. Every game of checkers, chess, cards, arm-wrestling, had always ended in the same way, with her father gloating and Emma sulking and feeling like a nothing.

It hadn't even been being beaten. That wasn't it. It had been the look on her father's face. It had been the gleam in his eye, as though once again, by beating his daughter, he had proven something. But what? What did you prove if you beat a four-year-old at checkers?

She remembered something her father used to do when she was very small.

He would sit down and make a circle with his arms. He would make her stand inside that circle. He would tell her to feel his muscles to see how strong he was. She would do that. He would then say, "Try to get out. Try to break through."

She remembered trying with all her might, pushing against his arms which ran like steel bands around her body. She would push and sweat and finally scream. He would laugh. "See," he'd say. "See how strong I am!" He would be exultant, laughing as she screamed, proud to busting of his power.

She let the humiliation of those moments fall into her. She felt the frustration, the helplessness, the rage. She wanted to cry, feeling it. She felt like a nothing.

He was sitting in that room, beaten. If she had done this, what would he do to her?

Terror struck her heart, climbed her throat, forced a constriction of a scream.

She was a small helpless dot of terror, spinning through space alone.

She thought of the times she had lain in bed at night and wanted to kill her father. If he knew, if he only knew what she had felt all these years, he would certainly want to kill her. He could kill her, that was the difference.

Would being beaten like this make him want to? She thought of herself the night before, screaming at him and telling him she was bored with his stories of his life.

Oh, God. Her heart sank. He knows, she thought, he knows I'm out to get him, and he's going to get me.

This is the low point of my life, she thought. If I even get up out of this chair, it will be a miracle. How can I ever walk into that room and face my father? I'll be terrified. I'll have to sit here in this chair the rest of my life.

"Emma," she heard her mother call, "dinner is ready."

Emma got up, without thinking, and went to the door.

● ●

Willie came dancing through the front door. After the rehearsal, Dipsey had taken him to a place down the block for a soda. Willie had been full of questions about all he had seen. Dipsey had answered them, laughing and every now and then punching Willie on the arm. Dipsey had said, "You're a real little hoofer, man." Willie had held this to his heart all the way home.

He had danced halfway into the living room before he saw his mother and father sitting there.

He saw his father's eyes. His knees began to tremble. He stopped where he was, dropping his books.

"Hello, dear," said his mother. She was smiling, but she looked nervous.

Uh-oh, thought Willie, here it comes. He wanted to run back to the door, out of the building, back to Dipsey. He wanted to have never come home.

"Come and tell us all about it," said his mother.

His father was looking out the window again, as if he hated the river and wanted to kill it.

"Was it as wonderful as you thought it would be? Was it hard?"

"Yes, mam," said Willie. He didn't know what to do. He could hear that his mother was on his side, but he could also hear that she was afraid. She must be as afraid of his father as he was.

In his pocket was a piece of paper he had to get his father to sign before tomorrow. How could he do that? He looked at his father's bulk. I can't ask him, he thought. The whole thing is going to fly out of my hands because I'm too scared to ask him.

I have to, he thought. I just have to. I don't care what happens. If I don't get to go back to rehearsal, I'll kill myself.

"Dad?" He said this so softly he could barely hear it himself. Louder, he repeated, "Dad?"

His father turned his head slowly, rather as a lion does.

"Yes?" His voice was deep.

"I have something I have to ask you."

"Ask your mother," said his father, and turned his head back to the window in the same slow way.

"William!" said his mother. She seemed shocked. "Willie, run and wash your hands now. Dinner is almost ready. Whatever you have to ask your father can wait until after dinner."

Willie ran, liberated, to his room. Once inside, with the door closed, he felt his heart fill up again with the joy, the excitement, the overwhelming love he had felt all afternoon.

● ●

Willie was dancing all over the dining room. He was doing some crazy step up and down, up and down, and around the table. It looked like a cakewalk.

Mr. Sheridan loped in from the living room, easing himself into his chair as though his body hurt. He neither said anything nor looked at Willie, who was orbiting the table like something in outer space.

"Sit down, dear," said Mrs. Sheridan. Willie sat, if what he did could be called sitting, since he continued moving even though he was on a chair.

"I learned six new steps today," he said wildly. "I learned to do a back flip too and—"

"What's for dinner?" interrupted his father in a heavy voice.

"Pot roast," said Mrs. Sheridan.

"—and I learned how the curtain goes up and down, and a little bit about lights—"

"And roast potatoes and gravy?" Mr. Sheridan sounded as though he were asking what time the funeral was.

Emma went off into a courtroom, a summer courtroom, its wide windows open all the way, the participants in the trial sweating and wiping their faces with handkerchiefs.

"The State of New York against Ms. Emancipation Sheridan on a charge of first-degree murder."

"Well, Emma," said her father in a sepulchral voice, "how was school today?"

"Fine," said Emma, helping herself to gravy. She had been through so much that for a minute she couldn't remember school at all.

"We went to get a soda afterwards," said Willie, rolling his eyes at his father without turning his head. "Dipsey and me."

Mr. Sheridan ignored him, continuing to eat in a steady way, looking pained.

"That's nice, dear," said Mrs. Sheridan.

"Did you or did you not plot the death of your own father, not one night but many nights?"

"The thought is not the deed," said Emma to the judge. She wore what she had come to think of as her working clothes: conservative pants suit, large flamboyant hat.

She was, in this fantasy, her own attorney, representing herself. The saying "He who is his own lawyer has a fool for a client" ran through her mind, to no avail.

"Your honor, I would like to plead not guilty."

"What is your defense?"

"There's no corpus delicti."

"You are aware, are you not, Counselor Sheridan, that the absence of a body does not necessarily mean you are cleared of these charges."

"Your honor, may it please the court, he's sitting right over there." She pointed at her father sitting in the back row of the courtroom.

"Get your finger out of my face and pass the gravy," said Mr. Sheridan.

Emma came back to reality with a bump, pulled her finger back, and passed the gravy.

"Dipsey picked you up after school, didn't he?" asked Mrs. Sheridan. Her voice was shaking.

It's making her nervous, thought Emma. She feels the way I did the other night after I yelled at him. She's afraid.

"Yup," said Willie.

"Yes, mam," corrected Mr. Sheridan. He continued to shovel food into his mouth, never looking up.

"And did he stay with you the whole rehearsal or did he wander off?"

"No, mam. He was right there. He made me sit next to him when we had a break. You know, when they want to have a break, you know what the director says?"

Mrs. Sheridan shook her head. She gave Mr. Sheridan a quick, worried look.

"He says, 'Take five,' and that means—"

"Pass the potatoes," said Mr. Sheridan loudly.

"Oh, William," said Mrs. Sheridan in a sad little voice.

"What? All I said was pass the potatoes. What's the matter with that?" Mr. Sheridan looked like a balloon about to get a pin stuck in it.

"And you know what shtick means?" said Willie, his voice rising. "And piece of business? And downstage and upstage and stage right and stage left and—"

"Let's have some peace and quiet around here," bellowed Mr. Sheridan.

He was so loud that Martha, leaving the room, almost dropped the serving platter.

"Dad," said Willie, in a sturdy little way, "I have something for you to sign."

"Sign?" Mr. Sheridan seemed affronted.

"You have to sign this thing with my agent. I'm too young to sign anything."

"Oh, is that so?" Mr. Sheridan leaned back in his chair and gave Willie a big smile. "So you finally need your old dad, do you?"

"Well, no, Mama could sign." Willie looked at his father uncertainly.

"Oh, is that so? Well, we'll just see what anybody signs. Nobody signs anything around here until I read it. Is that clear?"

Willie nodded. Now that he'd asked, he started to eat. He realized he was starving.

"And furthermore, if you're too young to sign something, you'd think it would occur to you that you're too young to be working." Mr. Sheridan seemed immensely pleased with himself.

"Dear. We'll discuss this after dinner, I think, don't you?" Mrs. Sheridan looked petrified of her husband and yet very definite at the same time.

Mr. Sheridan gave his wife a long, hard look. Emma and Willie watched, their heads turning back and forth between their parents.

Emma thought, he doesn't like her either. He doesn't like me or my mother. Maybe he doesn't like females. But he doesn't like Willie either, so what does that mean? Maybe he doesn't like people at all.

Do I like people? she asked herself with wonder. She had never thought of this before. She preferred books, she was aware of that, and she preferred being alone, but the idea that she simply didn't care for people in a sort of wholesale way had never entered her mind.

She imagined herself in a world with no people. She saw herself wandering down a street in New York, a street which was ordinarily full of people, a street now totally empty. She went into a building. There was no one there. She went out again, then into an office building. No one. She went up in the elevator to the highest floor. She looked down into empty streets. She was the only person in the world. A noise reached her.

She was screaming. She was sitting at the dinner table screaming her head off.

She stopped abruptly. Everyone was looking at her.

"Emma!" said Mrs. Sheridan. Emma looked at her blankly. "You see there, William. This is upsetting everybody. It's all this bickering. We can't have this kind of thing going on every night at the dinner table."

"What happened?" Martha burst through the door.

"It's all right," said Mrs. Sheridan.

"Sounded like you saw a mouse or something," said Martha, hanging around the door, not certain whether to go or stay.

"No. It's nothing. You can clear away now, Martha."

They sat in silence while Martha cleared the table.

Emma felt stunned at herself, and somehow ashamed. My emotions are spilling out all over the place. I don't know what to make of myself.

It's because there's no place to go. I can't go to my father. God knows, I can't go to my mother. I can't even go to Harrison Carter.

She looked at her father. He turned into a big rock right in front of her eyes. Her mother was a smaller, thinner rock. They're not going to change, she thought suddenly. No matter how much I need them to change, they're not going to.

They are going to be the way they are the rest of their lives. She saw them sitting, in this same way, in ten, twenty years.

Willie would be different, bigger for one thing, and then, finally, a grown man.

She, Emma, would be different, but they would be the same. They would always be the same.

"That's what wrong," she said aloud.

"What?" said Mrs. Sheridan quickly.

"Nothing," said Emma.

"Emma, do you feel all right?" asked her mother.

"Sure."

Mrs. Sheridan got up from the table, came to Emma, and felt her forehead. "You don't feel flushed," she said. "Do you have a sore throat?"

"No."

"No, mam," said Mr. Sheridan.

"No, mam," said Emma.

During this, her mind raced. What's wrong is trying to change them. They are not going to change. But I can change. I can change myself.

I can see them. I can see they're not going to change.

She jumped up from the table and started out the door.

"Emma," said Mrs. Sheridan. Emma turned back.

"Ask if you may be excused."

"May I be excused?"

"Yes, you may," said Mrs. Sheridan. "You don't feel sick, do you?"

Emma shook her head. Her mind was going so fast she didn't want to lose track of her thoughts by talking.

"Are you going to do your homework now? You don't want any dessert?"

Emma nodded to one and shook her head to the other. She had no desire to eat. The idea, in fact, was sickening.

"All right, dear." Mrs. Sheridan sounded bewildered.

Dismissed, Emma fled. She went to her room, closed the door, and sat down in her chair. Now to understand this, she said to herself, now to really understand this.

She got a piece of paper and a pencil from her desk. I must be organized about this, she thought, and I must calm down or I will lose my train of thought.

It seemed, for some reason, a hard thing to hold in her mind. She fell back into a familiar pattern.

"The State of New York against Parents."

Emancipation Sheridan, as District Attorney, stood up.

"Your honor, the prosecution opens its case—"

"Excuse me, Counselor, but what is the charge?" asked the judge.

"Breach of promise," said Emancipation Sheridan.

"Improper," said the judge.

"Eminently proper," said Emancipation Sheridan.

"Parents, by virtue of becoming parents, promise to love and accept their children. They do neither."

"Throw her out," said the judge.

I will always lose, thought Emma. I will be a loser in life, as I am in my dreams.

The judge was gesturing toward the back of the courtroom. "Mr. Sheridan," he said, "come forward and take this young woman's place. You know what you're doing. She doesn't. Bailiff, take her from the courtroom."

Emma watched her father come forward with a smug look on his face. She felt the bailiff take her arm. She felt herself propelled from the courtroom. When the courtroom door closed behind her, she woke up.

That's it. If the whole world is my father, I will always lose. I may grow up, I may become a lawyer, I may have a case in court, but I will always lose.

Unless I change.

How can I do that?

She was stumped. Why do I lose? Is losing inevitable? "Nothing is inevitable unless we refuse to look at it," she remembered seeing on a poster. Or was it, "unless we refuse to face it." Face what?

I'm facing that I'm a loser. What more can I do?

Why bit itself into her brain like a small spider. Why am I a loser? She sat very still.

Because it pleases my father. The thought flooded over her. She felt relief, a horrible kind of relief, but relief nevertheless.

She thought again of her father looking like a rock, not just a rock, but a huge boulder, a mountainous expanse of rock settled into the land, never moving.

It pleases him because he can go on seeing me the way he wants to see me, he doesn't have to change any ideas he has. He thinks women don't have good enough minds to be lawyers. He's said so. He tells stories about women lawyers in court and he laughs at them. My mother laughs too. They like to think that.

If I become a good lawyer, he'll have to change what he thinks. He won't be pleased at all.

But, still, when I hate him so, why would I want to please him?

I want him to love me.

This thought went through Emma like a hurricane, leaving her, afterward, as peaceful as a green lawn after a storm.

Oh, I do not, she said to herself then, but she knew she was lying.

Yes. I want him to love me and he won't. He just won't.

Her brain felt exhausted. She leaned over and turned on the television, picking up her homework at the same time.

● ●

Emma put down her book only once during the next

hour, and that was to think, who am I kidding? I'm only eleven years old. I can't move out. I have no money. I'm trapped here. I might as well be a slave. Who am I kidding, saying I will change? She remembered then: INNER PROGRESS BEFORE OUTER PROGRESS.

Did this apply? Yes. If she could stop wanting her father to love her, she would stop being a mess to please him, because if she stopped wanting him to love her, she wouldn't care if she pleased him or not.

There was a knock on her door. "Emma?" her mother said from the other side.

She got up and opened the door. Her mother came in.

"Emma, I'd like to talk to you a minute."

"Okay."

Her mother sat down on the bed. Emma went back to her chair.

"Emma, I'm worried about you. I see that you're very upset."

"Who, me?"

"Don't pretend, dear. It was obvious at dinner that you're upset. Now, what is troubling you?"

Obvious, yes, thought Emma. It's obvious that you don't love me any more than he does. It's obvious that you're not going to change either.

"Answer me, dear. Is something at school troubling you?"

Emma shook her head.

"Well. I didn't think so. You always make such good grades. What is it, then?"

"Mama, I want to be a lawyer when I grow up. What do you think of that?"

"Why, Emma, I think that's just fine. I mean, I think if a woman can raise her children and take care of her husband, then I think it's admirable if she also wants to go out and have a profession."

"I don't have any children, Mama," said Emma.

"I know, dear, I mean, after you are married—"

"I'm not getting married, Mama."

"Oh, well, now, you're a little young to be saying things like that. You wait until you're a little older. You'll see. You'll feel different."

"If you mean sex, I didn't say I didn't intend to have sex. I said I didn't intend to get married."

"Emma!" Mrs. Sheridan's expression was one of total amazement. "You don't know what you're saying."

"Mama, if I turned out to be a woman who lived in a way you didn't like, would you still love me?"

"Why . . ." Mrs. Sheridan began to splutter. "Emma, what, why of course, but you can't—"

"I can and I will," said Emma. "I can decide my life."

"You can't just decide to do anything you want. You can't—for instance, you can't break the law. You can't run through red lights whenever you feel like it."

I don't think we're even in the same conversation, thought Emma. What is she talking about, red lights?

"Mama, I saw you help Willie. Will you help me now?"

"Oh, darling, certainly. What can I help you with?"

"I want you to tell Dad that I want to be a lawyer."

"Emma, you can't be a lawyer at eleven."

"I am aware of that," said Emma, getting another surprised look from Mrs. Sheridan. "He could help me, though. He could teach me. He could give me a head start over everybody else. He could show me how to look up precedents, he could explain things to me. He could stop acting like he's acting."

"I don't know what you mean."

"You do too know what I mean. He hates me."

"Oh, darling, how absurd. Your father loves you."

Emma shook her head. There was no way around their crazy thinking. They think what they like to think, and what they don't like to think they just don't think that.

"In other words, you helped Willie, but you won't help me?"

"Honey, I'll help you in any way I can. This thing with Willie is something entirely different. It was just a matter of a misunderstanding with your father, and it's been cleared up."

"A misunderstanding!" Emma clapped her hand to her head.

"Don't get agitated," said Mrs. Sheridan.

"But can't you see that it's all the same thing? Willie

wants to do a girl's thing, and I want to do a boy's thing, and our father hates both of us."

"That is absolutely absurd. Dancing is not a girl's thing, as you call it—although being a lawyer, I guess you're right, that is a boy's thing. I agree with your father. I don't think you'll be happy that way either, and I think you should stop all this nonsense. Just stop thinking about it."

"You're in the Middle Ages." Emma stood up and walked around. She didn't want to look at her mother.

"I may very well be in the Middle Ages, as you say, I don't care about that. I know that I've been very happy being a wife and raising you two. I don't go along with this liberation thing all the way. I think a lot of women are happy doing what they're doing, and that if anything is making them unhappy, it's all this agitation about women not being fullfilled if they don't have a career. I think that's true for some women, but not for others."

Emma stopped walking. "How about me? I'm not going to be happy being a wife."

"Emma, nobody is doing anything to you. Nobody is making you get married at eleven." Mrs. Sheridan looked arch. "I doubt that anybody has even asked you!"

Emma felt, suddenly, like a huge lump of clay, ungainly, unattractive, in fact, ugly. She sat down. She fell into despair.

"I think you kids these days get yourselves all worked up over nothing."

I have to hold on to this train of thought, Emma said to herself, feeling mush-brained. Why had it all seemed so clear before *she* came into the room?

"He is too doing something to me," she said loudly, everything coming back to her. "He's ruining what I think of myself!"

"What are you talking about?"

"And you are too! You both make me feel like I'm a big lump that doesn't know what I'm talking about, and I do! I do know what I'm talking about!"

"What *are* you talking about?" repeated Mrs. Sheridan.

"I'm talking about me and what I think of myself. I think I'm some big fat loser."

"Oh, so it's what you think of yourself, so we're not doing anything. You're doing it to yourself!"

Boy, thought Emma, that takes the cake. Anything to get them off the hook. Anything to make them look good. *They're not going to change* came insistently into her brain like a sad tune. They're not going to change, I have to change; they're not going to change, I have to change; like a hurdy-gurdy played for a monkey on a summer afternoon.

"Forget it," she mumbled.

"What?"

"I said never mind."

"I think you should give some thought to what I've said tonight. I think you're thinking about a lot of things you don't have any business thinking about at eleven years old. I think you ought to do your homework and get to sleep. You're very overwrought tonight. Do you have your period?"

"No." Emma covered her eyes. If there was one thing she hated to talk about or even think about, it was that.

"Couldn't you see"—Emma took one last desperate chance—"couldn't you see tonight that he even hated *you*?"

"No. Your father doesn't hate me." Mrs. Sheridan smiled. She put her hand on her daughter's head. "Is that what's bothering you? Do you think he hates me? Well, I can see why you're upset. Did you worry we might get a divorce?"

"Oh, for God's sake," said Emma. Her mother was way off the track.

"Don't talk like that. Now, was that what was bothering you? Well, I'll tell you something, Emma. Your father may be just the slightest bit upset, but that's temporary and it doesn't upset me, it doesn't even upset Willie. The person it seems to be upsetting the most is you. I think that's because you're getting the wrong things in your head about this. It doesn't mean divorce. It doesn't mean your father hates me. It doesn't mean your father hates you. It doesn't mean any of those things."

"Okay," said Emma wearily.

"What's that?"

"Okay, okay." There was no point in talking about

it any longer, because no matter how long she talked, there wouldn't be anyone to understand her.

She thought of Goldin. Goldin would understand her, so would Saunders. Ketchum was another matter. Ketchum looked as though she had such a hard time just getting through the day that understanding would be beyond her.

Emma sat, silently laughing at Ketchum. Her shoulders were shaking.

"Are you crying?" asked her mother.

"What? No," said Emma, still shaking. "I'm laughing."

"What are you laughing at?" asked her mother with somewhat exaggerated politeness.

"I'm laughing at how silly I am," said Emma.

"I think that's a good, positive attitude," said her mother. "I'm glad to see you haven't lost your sense of humor." She opened the door. "If you want to talk to me again about this, Emma, please know that you can at any time."

Emma's shoulders started shaking again. Her mother didn't seem to notice, because she went out and shut the door without saying anything further.

"I'm silly because I've been talking to the wrong people," said Emma aloud to the empty room.

She saw herself in full-dress uniform addressing her troops. Saunders' uniform was quite gaudy. Goldin's was exactly like Saunders'. Ketchum had on a uniform too big for her, its hat covering her eyes completely.

"Troops!" shouted Emma in her head. *"We* are the only ones who can change! Change is with *us!"*

Ketchum saluted, tripped, and fell over.

"Rats," said Emma. "Male images. I'm sick of male images, armies, uniforms, salutes, kowtowing. I'm sick of males altogether."

She thought of herself actually calling Saunders and arranging a meeting after school.

I know I'm right, she thought. I hope they agree with me, because, if they don't, I'll have to do it all myself.

● ●

"I looked up the word in the dictionary," said Emma. She was holding the piece of paper on which she had written the definition. The wind from the river flipped it a little as she talked. Saunders, Goldin, and Ketchum faced her, listening.

"Here it is," she said, "and I think it's a good word to describe what I'm talking about."

"Changeling?" said Saunders. "I thought it meant some kid in an Irish fairy tale, stolen away by the leprechauns."

"I guess that's what they mean in this first definition," said Emma. "What I mean is, somebody who is young and somebody who changes."

They'd been sitting on the bench for over an hour. Emma had felt completely inarticulate when she began to talk to them about her idea. She didn't know what it was about ideas, but they could seem so simple when they came to you as a feeling, then when you tried to put them into words and tell someone else, they seemed impossibly complicated.

"I mean that nobody's family is going to change. This means if we don't want to go on feeling the way we're feeling, then *we* have to change."

"I get it, sort of," said Goldin.

"But, you know, it sounded like the Children's Army does change things." Saunders seemed puzzled; not angry, just confused.

"It doesn't really change anything. I mean, do you really believe, like take a kid whose father is beating him up, and the committee comes in and everything, and this guy, the father, says he'll change. Do you really believe he doesn't swat that kid the minute the committee leaves the house?"

"No," said Saunders. "That's why, in bad cases like that, they get the kid removed. They get him some other place to live."

"Exactly," said Emma.

Everybody looked at her. "Clear as mud," said Saunders. "What are you saying?"

"I'm saying fathers don't change and mothers don't change. It's up to us to change." Emma had said it as

well as she could. She couldn't think of any other way
to say it.

Ketchum was nodding slowly. "Mine won't change,"
she said.

"I never thought about it," said Saunders.

There she goes again, thought Emma. If she didn't
think of it, it annoys her. She's only enchanted by her
own mind.

"My father certainly won't change," said Goldin.

"Read the definition," said Saunders, playing for
time.

"Okay, but it really doesn't apply. I don't know why
I brought it. I mean, I just like the word because I think
it describes somebody young changing." Saunders had
gotten everybody interested in the definition now, so
there was nothing for Emma to do but read it.

"Changeling, noun," read Emma. "Definition 1 is a
child surreptitiously or unintentionally substituted for
another. Definition 2a is archaic, and is a disloyal person." Emma looked around.

"What's definition 2b?" asked Saunders.

"Oh, nothing. It means nothing," said Emma.

Saunders grabbed the piece of paper. "Definition 2b
is an imbecile," she read aloud. She laughed, a great big
laugh.

Goldin covered her face and Ketchum squealed off
into a series of high giggles that finally had everybody
turned in her direction.

"Oh, for God's sake," said Emma. "I told you guys this didn't mean anything." She felt despondent. Why was she trying this, anyway? These goons would never understand what she was talking about. They were still laughing. "Listen, to hell with it. I mean, I'm going to do it, but you guys can do what you want."

They stopped laughing. "I think this all sounds good," said Goldin. Saunders turned to her in surprise. "I think about my father and I know he's never going to change." She looked straight into Emma's eyes. "I don't understand how *I'm* supposed to, that's all."

"I meant that we—I thought that if we—" Emma stopped. Damn it, it was embarrassing. "I thought we could try and help each other."

There was silence. Emma wanted to grab back every word and run out of the park. She never wanted to see these girls again. Obviously, she had made a fool of herself.

Saunders nodded. "Like a consciousness-raising group?"

Emma nodded. Was it possible they understood?

Goldin and Ketchum were nodding too. "I see it," said Goldin. "But I don't see how to change."

"I don't either," said Ketchum in a woeful voice. Emma figured she was seeing herself face to face with her uncle of an afternoon.

"Well, for instance, your uncle," said Emma. Ketchum jumped. "Say he comes to the door."

Ketchum seemed about to jump out of her skin at the thought.

"What does he say he's come there for?" asked Emma.

"He says he'll just wait for my mother to come home from work," said Ketchum in a quavering voice.

"Okay, so you leave," said Emma.

"Where would I go?" asked Ketchum.

"That's not the point. He's not going to follow you, is he? I mean, he's said he's come there to wait, so he won't come with you, because that would make a liar out of him. So it doesn't matter where you go. Come to my house if you want to." Emma felt exhilarated. The whole thing was much easier to explain when you had examples.

Ketchum smiled broadly. Her braces glinted in the sun.

"What about my father?" asked Goldin.

"Your father," said Saunders, "is a lost cause. He thinks those boys are great and he's never going to think you're anything, because you're a girl."

"Well," said Goldin, "I can't change that."

"No, but you can stop wanting him to change," said Saunders.

Emma felt like the top of her head would fly off. Saunders got it, the whole thing. "That's what I mean," said Emma loudly. "That's just what I'm talking about. We have to stop waiting around for them to love us!"

"Hey," said Saunders. "You know, you're right. That's

just what I do. I keep waiting for my mother to say, 'I think it's wonderful that you want to be a scientist.' I keep waiting for her to think it's as wonderful as I think it is.''

"That ain't never going to happen," said Emma, thinking of her own father. Never, ever, would he look at her and say he thought it was a swell idea, her being a lawyer, never, if she waited a million years.

"I think we've got something here," said Saunders.

What do you mean *we,* thought Emma.

"I think we ought to meet once a week," continued Saunders, "or more—every day if we have to—and talk about what we feel and see if we can figure out solutions, see if we can help each other. I even like the name. Let's call ourselves the Changelings!"

Can you beat that, thought Emma. In one more minute she'll give herself the credit for thinking of the whole thing.

"What I was originally thinking of when I first thought of this," said Emma slowly, letting her words sink in, "was that we would also enlarge the group, and start other groups, so that, finally, when people get to be ten or eleven, or even earlier, it would be a natural thing for people to belong to a group like this."

"Great," said Saunders, as though Emma had finally contributed something.

"Why don't we get sweat shirts," said Goldin excitedly.

"No!" said Emma. "This should be secret."

"Like the Army?" asked Goldin. "Hey, are we going to belong to the Children's Army?"

"I don't know how I feel about that," Emma said importantly. "I spoke to Harrison Carter."

"You did?" asked Goldin, obviously impressed. Saunders looked put out by the news.

"I'm not sure what I think of the operation," said Emma. "They accomplish a lot, I know that."

"It's not the same thing as this," said Saunders. "One thing doesn't have anything to do with the other."

"Yeah," said Goldin. "They're two different things."

"I think," said Emma, "that the first meeting of the Changelings should come to order."

"Who made you president?" asked Saunders swiftly.

"She thought of it," said Goldin.

That Goldin is a good kid, thought Emma, as she continued: "I think the first thing on the agenda is for each person to discuss how she plans to be different at dinner tonight."

"Motion passed," said Ketchum wildly.

They began to talk. They talked all afternoon.

● ●

That night, at dinner, Emma waited until dessert was served to make her announcement.

She waited patiently, watching Willie try to tell what

had happened that day at rehearsal. She watched her mother being nervous. She watched her father retreating more and more into silence, eating faster and faster. She watched her mother watching her father.

When Martha placed a piece of chocolate cake in front of her, Emma pushed it away and said, "I'm going to be a lawyer when I grow up."

"Oh, for Christ's sake! Can't we have a peaceful dinner around here?" said her father loudly. He jerked his cake closer to him and shoved his fork down into it.

"Stop saying things just to upset your father!" said Mrs. Sheridan.

"Women lawyers are idiots! They're the laughing-stock of any group of lawyers. I think any woman who tries to be a lawyer is a damned fool!" Mr. Sheridan glared at Emma.

"That," said Emma, "is your problem, not mine." To herself she added, And frankly, Daddy, I don't give a damn.

She shook with silent laughter. Wait till I tell them tomorrow how these two looked when I said that.

Just wait.

PB
Fit
C-2 Fitzhugh, Louise
    Nobody's family is going
to change.

PAPERBACK

DATE DUE			
NOV 1 4 1983			

Organization

MS-10/77

A PUBLIC SERVICE MESSAGE FROM DELL PUBLISHING CO., INC.